LOUNGE ACT

LOUNGE ACT

A NOVEL

Adrienne Reiter

Cotton Wolf Publishing

Library of Congress Control Number: 2018946808

Paperback ISBN: 978-0-9963481-5-7
eBook ISBN: 978-0-9963481-6-4

Cover design by Cecilia Arthursson

www.cottonwolfpublishing.com

Printed in the United States of America
1 2 3 4 5 6 7 8 9 10

For Norma and friends who hear the same tune,
like Tom and Leo.

"We're so trendy we can't even escape ourselves."
                                                  -Kurt Cobain

LOUNGE ACT

PROLOGUE

Little Chris took a break from the two women to seek out more pills. He loved the way they made his girlfriend and her pretty friend from LA respond. Eyeing his naked body in the bathroom mirror, he preened. Little was a misnomer.

It only took a few drama--free days for Chris to really tie one on. Donatus and Cherry probably had even better stuff stashed in one of their bedside tables. Their so called "goody-drawers." Being a rock star was great, but being a rock star's friend and on the payroll was fantastic! He never envied Donatus and Cherry as they sweated under the demanding heat of stage lights, or fought off swarms of fans that would descend on them like locusts. Chris looked around the cavernous bedroom filled with designer name brands hiding designer glam drugs. He certainly liked using their stuff. He found more pills in the master bathroom's medicine cabinet. As he turned to leave the second floor, a shot rang out overhead. His heart sank into the pit of his stomach. It had begun.

1

Lifting my head up off the table a piece of paper stuck to my face with either sweat or saliva. I peeled it off not caring which one. Running on little to no sleep, I pushed away from my desk and rolled my chair back toward the wall. I wished for more Go Pills. Where was he? It'd been two years since dad died. I was prepared for an Easter morning alone, but alone in my office waiting with anticipation? Where the hell was James, and what the hell had happened?

A motorcycle roared into our Santa Monica office's driveway. Finally. I couldn't wait to hear the news. If it was good we would get out of here. My tip better have worked.

Steam no longer rose from the coffee cup on my desk. Who ever thought a chain of cafés could become so popular? I shook my empty pill bottle hoping I'd missed one. The pharmacy wouldn't refill my usual pick me up for one more week and coffee wasn't cutting it. I spun my chair away from the doorway so he wouldn't see me. I listened to hurried footsteps made by heavy boots. The door opened and shut.

"Oh, good." He sighed, breathless.

"James," I spun my chair back around.

"Holy shit." James gripped the lapel of his leather jacket.

"You're late."

"There was traffic. I wasn't expecting traffic on Easter Sunday."

"This is LA There's always traffic."

"I only just moved from Philly a few months ago."

"You don't have traffic in Philadelphia?"

Looking at him from the neck down one would think he was twenty-five, but scrolling up to his face made him an easy mid-thirties. The nephew of the private investigator who owned the company, James has done some hard living. Formerly an attorney, he transitioned to bounty hunter after he went straight and now, like me, he was a P.I. at his Uncle Joe Stack's firm. Not an unusual career jump.

I could smell James from my chair as he shed his leather jacket; a not unpleasant compound of motor oil, leather, pine-ish shave gel, and spicy deodorant. We fell into each other's beds while working our first case in New York together. His scent hadn't changed.

"Please tell me you were able to get in touch with Griselda."

"Yup, I rode my bike right out to the front of that asshole's apartment complex. He was home, and he tried to lay low. He didn't turn the kid over until the cops came. How did you know he would be there?"

"I was worried Jose had fled back to Tijuana with the kid. My real estate license and what few connections I have left on the force still give me unregulated access to property records. That dump of an apartment you staked out was the forwarding address."

"At least we got the kid back to his mother."

I was only in the office on this holiday weekend to wrap up a missing persons case. With my database access, I got the kid home for the family's Easter party. That felt good. Too bad it didn't pay the bills. I was going to have to take a second mortgage on my little house in the Valley. James' Uncle Joe was going to pull our funding if we didn't get more paying clients fast.

Soon I would have to get rid of the hotrod, the only thing I had left of my dad. Who was I kidding? I'd live in that damned Impala before I'd let it go. I thought of my dog and the television waiting for me. I'd even have time to hit the gym on the way home. I began scooping up my long blonde hair into a ponytail. I caught James eyeing me thoughtfully. I signaled for us to go before he had a chance to ask me out again, but I could tell he wasn't giving up by the intent look in his eye; the same look that had brought me to bed with him. I knew better than to mess around with a co-worker twice, especially a psycho bitch magnet like James.

"Has your crazy stalker ex tried calling you again? I still can't believe she followed you out here to California."

Just when he was about to open his mouth the phone rang. I lifted my index finger.

"Now who calls on Easter? Hold on just a second James. Stacks Private Investigators, can I help you?"

A woman's voice faltered and rasped on the other end, exhaling into the receiver.

"I'm sorry. I couldn't get that."

"I need to hire a private investigator." She coughed. "It's about a stolen credit card."

"If someone is unlawfully using your credit card, maybe the police are the better people to call."

I was tempted to hang up. Then she said, "Well, you know, my husband and I are kind of famous, and we need to get this done right away."

I scribbled the name on my legal notepad as James leaned over my shoulder. I looked back at him, and his cheeks and neck sparked red. He hadn't even bothered with the ancient ninja art of peering down women's shirts.

He looked back down and read the rock star's name crowded by other notes on the yellow paper. "You've got to be kidding me!"

James grabbed a People magazine and opened it up to its headline article: "Coma Scare for Bliss Front Man Donatus Sun." I flipped through the rag. Donatus had accidentally OD'd in Italy just a few weeks earlier. There was a picture of a blonde sitting on the edge of an ambulance looking frantic. Her red lips were smeared, her mascara running down her cheeks. Her shoulder length platinum blonde hair was unkempt in a wild array of assaulted baby doll curls. A short black slip clung loosely to her torso under a plush open jacket. The caption below simply said,

"Wife Cherry Starlet."

"And to whom am I speaking please?"

"Cherry, Cherry Starlet. I'm at The Peninsula Hotel. Can you come over today? As soon as possible?"

Why me, because I answered the phone? Probably. How many other private investigators could she have called flipping through the Los Angeles phone book before one picked up on Easter Sunday? My guess was quite a few.

"What room number?"

2

"I didn't peg you as someone who could get star struck."

James tried to shrug, but his shoulders did more of an excited shudder. "Bliss is one of my favorite bands."

I was getting a kick out of watching a bright-eyed James on the edge of his seat as we entered Beverly Hills. Cherry Starlet was all big tits and red lips, and he was about to see her in person.

A bellman took us up to her room and escorted us to the door. He knocked, and then backed away. After a minute and a half, the door swung open and a woman in white lingerie hanging on even whiter skin opened the door. A cigarette in one hand, Coca-Cola in the other, she sneered with smeared red lips. Her eyelashes were coated in so much mascara I thought I heard them clink as she blinked.

"You leak this to the press, and I'll sue the shit out of you," she said, then walked off. The back of her hair looked like she had been getting a vigorous workout right before she answered the door.

"I'm Brittany Wolfe. Nice to meet you, too," I said

looking at James as we followed her; the room was so dark we had to squint. James shut the door behind us. In the close air, the stale smell of cigarettes and the rancid scent from the food cart near the door were dueling with the sweet smell of perfume and body odor.

"Donatus escaped from rehab here in LA a couple of weeks ago. He bought a ticket back to Seattle, but nobody's seen him since." Cherry used a finger to open the curtains a crack. In the sliver of light, I could see through her negligee. She might as well have had nothing on.

The suite that would have been naturally light and airy was closed off and depressing. The sliver of southern California sun peeping through heavy dark curtains spotlighted Oriental rugs and light hardwood floors. With the living area windows open one would enjoy spacious garden-view balconies.

The windows were only cracked, the shades drawn, and the French doors were shut blocking access to the sitting room. It looked like there was additional access to the grounds' pools and gardens; most likely they would never be used.

Her silk and lace panties, thigh highs, and baby doll top were wrinkled and dirty, but I could tell by the hemlines they were very expensive. They were lived in. Grunge, the kinderwhore look, was an addition from riot grrrl bands. I had once watched an interview with Cherry in which she claimed it was she who single handedly began the trend.

Cherry turned in the window light. The grime of

11

old makeup and dried sweat formed dirty clots between her breasts and settled in the lines on her neck. She looked derelict in contrast to the opulent room.

She walked over to the bed and reclined, a filthy Venus with her cigarette and ashtray, as we took a seat on the large, deep couch opposite. James slumped like a padded leather jacket on an inadequate hanger, his face filled with disappointment.

She inhaled deeply then exhaled her smoke while staring up at the ceiling. "I called the credit card company and told them the card was stolen and they should cancel it."

"Was it?"

"What?"

"Stolen."

"No." Cherry exhaled, sat up, and looked at me through squinted eyes.

"Donatus' card wasn't stolen, but I had called the credit card company and canceled it so no one could use it. I needed to cut him off from his money somehow."

"I'm sure your husband has other ways of getting money," said James. I nodded, picking some white lint off my black blazer.

Cherry glared at James, then squinted her eyes at me while stubbing out her cigarette. "Are you kidding me? Donatus is helpless and doesn't have any friends. At least, no one that would loan him money. He only has the one credit card, I mean, he couldn't catch a fucking cab by himself."

Cherry pushing the idea that a modern rock God could be so helpless was absurd. James crossed his arms. He wasn't picking up what she was laying down either.

She lit another cigarette and tossed her lighter onto the counter next to the bed. Her fingers twitched. As the door to the room opened we all looked over. Cherry smiled as a woman let herself in with a room key.

"Hey," the woman eyed us with a sleepy smile, a crop top and low-rise jeans.

"Hey," Cherry slapped the redhead's thigh as she walked past us toward the shut off sitting room. She opened the doors just wide enough to slip through then shut the French doors behind her.

"That's my "drug dealer," Cherry made quotations with her fingers. "I need my medicine." Cherry got up on her knees, then to her feet. I could see the front of her entire sex as she stretched her legs across the bed, rose onto her knees, and hopped up to follow her friend.

James' grimaced face bespoke of the full-frontal view.

"According to Vanity Fair, Cherry is supposed to be in an in-house rehab holed up in a hotel," he said.

"There's reportage for you. She's a junky, so is the girl in there, and clearly no one is here to oversee this shit show."

"Yet we have a front row seat," James said.

Ten minutes later the two girls came sauntering back in. Cherry carried with her another lit cigarette and a soda pop can. I couldn't stop looking at her greasy tangled blonde mop. Is it possible to do so many drugs, your hair looks high? Both the girls' platinum bleached hair was oily at the scalp and dry at the ends, their eyes pinned and shinning bright. Cherry's friend melted into a love seat next to the bed, as Cherry resumed her reclined position.

"Listen, Donatus escaped from rehab, he bought a shotgun, and I just feel like something bad is going to happen. He's been suicidal for months now. Everybody knows it. Everybody thinks he's going to die." Cherry readjusted to sit on her knees, her feet crossed at the ankles. Her pinned eyes looked around. She stared through us more than at us.

I steadied myself not to look down past her bellybutton, feeling very square in my black blazer, jeans, and white t-shirt. James tried not to stare too closely either. What good are perky breasts when covered in sweat and grime?

Cherry sighed and rested her forehead in the palm if her hand. "We need to find him, now. Can't you contact the credit card company as my private investigators and find out what attempted activities have been on his canceled card?"

"Are you sure you need us for that?" I was familiar with the scenario. Once these celebrity personalities became pilled out narcotic messes they acted out a dream state. This woman was clearly very wealthy, with staff doing everything for her, and that's not real life. I couldn't tell if Cherry had even a tentative grasp on reality.

"Yes! Or why would I have called you?"

"I charge fifty bucks a phone call, a secretary would be cheaper."

"Fifty bucks per phone call?" Cherry laughed. "If you need more money, just ask. Like I give a shit."

"Wait a minute," James sounded as annoyed as I felt. A man with his own recovery problems tends to reserve very little patience for bullshit. "If he bought a shotgun and he's suicidal, then dealing with this credit card problem, that's the least important thing we could help you with."

"Well, that's where I want you to start."

I took in the red and gold floor-to-ceiling textiles and tried to reason with myself. A room like this had to be at least a grand and a half a night. How could canceling her millionaire husband's credit card give this woman any indication that she was cutting her husband off from his own funds?

Something was way off. I wasn't keen on the scent trail this rocker chick was sending us down. I glanced at the exploded armoire spilling out expensive fabric in the corner, designer handbags strewn about the room. It was the classic Los Angeles show of meaningless opulence. It's expensive, because it is. Meaningless spending resulting in wasted time and resources. Well, I needed access to resources. My business needed money.

"My partner and I will call up the credit card company and see what we can find. We suggest you do some digging of your own. Your husband's credit company will probably be more forth coming with information for you. Let's reconvene tomorrow."

"Alright, sounds good. Until tomorrow." Cherry rolled over to stub out her cigarette in the one crystal ashtray that wasn't overflowing. She picked up a piece of paper off the counter. "Brittany, here. This is Jessica Black's address. If Donatus is in Seattle, he's there. She's his drug dealer."

Back in the car I made a brief phone call. I was half shocked my car phone hadn't been shut off. I couldn't remember the last time I paid the bill. "I can't afford the minutes, call me at the Flamenco."

3

I pulled my black 327, four-barrel, V-8 engine, automatic, four-door, hardtop 1967 Chevy Impala into a lucky spot. Jimmy Hendrix's, *Across Town* stopped as I turned off my ignition. James and I dipped into The Flamenco, a crumbling old Hollywood hotel not without its charm in all its faded gold-chromed glory. The attached bar's wobbly counter smelled like a moldy bar rag that never knew soap. James and I took seats at the near-empty counter. It was almost 3 p.m.

"Hello and welcome. What's the deal, you two?" asked the towering hunched over bartender with a crooked black bow tie. He had used Just For Men on his head so much it gleamed like he got a shoeshine upside down.

"I'll have a Coors and a Makers."

"Soda water with lime for me." James rubbed the back of his neck and looked out towards the open exit.

I hadn't considered how being in Cherry's junky den might affect him. Our drinks looked doll sized in our bartender's mammoth hands. I poured beer on top of my embarrassment in the hope it would dissolve.

I took in the desolate bar and tried to imagine hanging around without a drink in my hand. The crown molding had recently been painted a jaunty red to de-uglify the place, but it was like sticking a red nose on a three-legged reindeer that had long lost its eyes, antlers, and tale. The place was oppressive in its ugliness. I didn't mind. It was one of the few bars left in Los Angeles where I could still afford a drink.

"Is there a Brittany Wolfe here?" a portly woman shouted from the entryway. Her hair was moose lacquered into a severe bun, and contrasted with her faded white and purple flower print dress and wood sandals.

"Over here."

"You have a phone call dear." I followed the older woman to the front desk adorned with a cigarette burning down in a black plastic ashtray.

"This is Brittany. What's the word in Seattle?"

"We've cased out Donatus' house. He's not there now, but he's in town. You want us to stake it out?" Tom huffed. I could hear the intake of a cigarette drag on the other end.

"No, his wife is jumpy, in the over medicated drug addled kind of way. Can you guys just keep your ear to the ground? Maybe shake things up and see what rises to the top? Check out this address, 2167 Soothie Lane, Apt. B." Must be a basement apartment. They always give shitty basement apartments letters instead of numbers. "It's near the Aurora Strip. It's Donatus' drug dealer's."

"Sure thing."

"And don't call Cherry's hotel. Something doesn't feel right. Call me here the same time tomorrow."

"Sure thing. Thanks, Brit. Talk soon."

I moved towards the bar. The bartender hovered over James, his lips pressed together moistly.

"I see your lady friend hasn't been back. She checking in with her old man to make sure you two won't be bothered?"

"No, and she's a colleague, not my lady."

"You looking for one? I know a few, young and not good with a dollar. They work hard for it."

"Sex isn't the most important thing in a man's life. I'm the old-fashioned type. I prefer money." James knocked back the rest of his soda and looked over the bartender's shoulder at the clock.

"Alright, but if not sex, what does a man need money for?" He let out a low bronchial chuckle.

"So, he can take a pilgrimage of repentance as a Franciscan Monk." James flashed the butt of his gun. "Pimping can get you five years."

"Oh, hell man." His eyes widened. The face under the black, stiff shiny hair was wiped clean of all smugness. "It was a joke, friend."

"Ready to head?" James looked over at me and rose off his barstool.

"We'll be back tomorrow." I waved at the low-level pimp.

"That's just swell," muttered the bartender as he moved dirt around the counter with a grey wet rag.

James frowned. "Why do we have to come here again?"

19

"Tom Depot, my northwest connect is paranoid about the high profile political cases I worked on in the LAPD. He's convinced my car and house phone could be tapped. Old hotels with switchboards are the hardest to listen in on. Trust me, there's no arguing with him."

Back in my car I unbuttoned my blazer to loosen up a bit. James tensed, and looked away. Sober, James had morals, my favorite virtue in a man. I leaned over letting my lips hover close to his and got an immediate response. He pressed himself into me hard; his hands gripped the side of my waist before climbing their way up. So, unethical.

I should have been keeping an eye on him. Not eyeing him. The guy I was dating wasn't into kissing. A finance guy and pathologically dispassionate, intimacy was foreign to him. I hadn't heard from him in weeks. To my complete non-surprise I didn't care.

James was raw, sensual, and easy to melt into, the perfect amount of rough as his stubble tickled your skin, then scratched you during the frantic pressure. His full mouth under his Romanesque nose pressed against yours was so soft in contradiction to the sharp edges of his cheekbones carving into your face. The combination never failed to send a spark down my spine to my toes.

His model good looks did make him a bit self-obsessed. Instead of partying James was now fitness crazed to the point of making my own daily workout look like mere maintenance, but being the envy of the women (and a few men) as we traveled around together made his vanity tolerable. I didn't know how he was elsewhere, but when we were together, he only had eyes for me. Too bad his past in the form of a Jersey girl with a hair-trigger temper followed him out to LA.

"Are you guys leaving?" A bleached woman in an old Mercedes missing hubcaps glared at us over her rolled down window.

"Yup."

"Take me home and I'll take you to breakfast," James grinned.

"Alpha will be happy to see you." I pulled out of the space, my engine roaring down the road as James gripped my thigh.

"Just pull over here and we'll switch spots."

"No way. No detours."

"Brittany, please?"

"No way!"

"I let you ride my Harley, and you dumped it!"

Damn thing was 900 pounds, and when it fell on me the rocky curb punctured the fuel tank. James wouldn't let me forget.

"Oh, alright." I was tired anyway. Pulling over on Hollywood Boulevard I let James get behind the wheel of the Impala. In the passenger seat, I rested my head against the window as he drove us to the Valley.

The Impala was rumbling up my little driveway by the time I opened my eyes. I forgot what a hypnotic quality sitting passenger side of the low rumbling car could have. I got out to open and shut the gate. Doubts on bringing him back here faded as I rolled the chain link fence shut so I could let out Alpha.

A reflection of light flashed across the street. It was just for a second, like someone holding a magnifying glass up to reflect the sun.

"James, stop." I motioned for him to come stand by me after he parked.

"What's up?"

"Do you see the grey car across the street? It's never been there before. There's someone inside, and I could swear they just put away binoculars." The figure wore sunglasses, a dark baseball cap, and a dark shirt. From the angle and distance, it was impossible to tell if it was a man or woman.

"So?"

"So, nobody parks there. It's across the street from the playground and overnight parking isn't allowed. I swear they sat up and pulled out binoculars as we arrived." I opened the gate and started to cross the street. The vehicle pulled out and drove away.

"Isn't that strange?"

"You're paranoid."

I reached through to the back of my mailbox – a few letters were sticking out - then closed the gate. My one-and a-half-bedroom Encino cottage was nestled between two large gated compounds. It was rumored that they were Century City Network types, but I'd never met them. I had only seen their Mercedes come and go. Between their security lights and my German Shepherd Pit mix I didn't need to shut my gate unless I was letting my dog roam the yard.

I opened my front door. The black and tan 120-

pound shepherd body with Pit Bull face came bounding out. She lifted her leg to pee on the one tree in front of the house. She never got the memo bitches were supposed to squat. Her butt wiggled as she nosed her hellos at James and me. James threw her ball back and forth as I unloaded the car. Alpha was friendly, but when I took her to the park parents motioned their kids to stay away. Handsome as she was fierce, her abnormally light Pit Bull blue eyes combined with her German Shepherd shading did give her the look of a hellhound.

It was an accident we met back when I was a police officer for LAPD. I found her as a small pup living off a bowl of dirty water and a rancid meat bone while tethered to a short metal chain staked to the ground. I could see all her ribs, and her chain was way too heavy for her feeble little body. The junkies living at the residence were too concerned with coping and selling dope to remember to feed her or change her water bowl. Terrified of human contact she tried to bite me as I unhooked her choker and picked her up. So malnourished, she could barely break the skin. When I put the pathetic thing in the back of my squad car my partner looked the other way.

We bonded quickly. It took two years to wean her off trying to crawl into my lap. Now she acted like a normal hyper working dog. Her Shepherd-Pit hybrid gave her a fearless presence, but every time she saw a chain or heard one rattle she began to shake and whimper.

James lifted the cloth leash off the front porch bench

and clipped into Alpha's collar. Her butt wiggled through the side gate as we exited to our tree lined walk. I thought I caught him looking around warily. The baggage following James went beyond weekly A.A. and NA meetings. I wondered if his ex tried phoning him again.

After the monster walk needed for the monster, I fed Alpha her kibble with skin from the fish I cooked the night before, and James and me the scallops, asparagus, and mashed potatoes I thought I would be eating alone. In the kitchen with food on the stove, I went through my letters; a few bills I'd soon be able to pay, a packet of useless coupons, and a silver- and gold-edged fancy invitation. I opened the invite to a gala book release event for my ex-boyfriend, Ryan Kemp. He'd done well for himself, and either this was a weird mistake, or he wanted me to know. Last I heard he was still dating that media whore heiress, Cynthia Khodorkovsky, famous for being wealthy and attention seeking.

"I'm hungry, what's taking so long?" You can take the trust fund away from the man, but you can't take the spoiled out of his tone. I put the invite away.

After dinner we washed up together, and enveloped each other. After wrapping me in a towel, James threw on his sweats and took Alpha out while I got ready. Tired, I was half asleep as I heard James enter the bedroom, shut the door, and Alpha grumble on the other side of it. James fell into my bed; the weight of his body slid me to him. We slept very little.

Our tender kissing led to hair pulling and nibbling.

After a teasing intensity for a few hours it culminated into the extreme rigor of a cheap, one-night stand. Some of the time, James would repeat the process. Tonight was one of those nights. I never could get over the shock of his intensity. James was an addict. After I pulled on my robe he held me close as he snored softly in my ear.

I awoke with a jolt. There wasn't the usual canine snoring coming from the edge of my bed. Where's my dog? Then I felt that familiar weight. James was the big spoon behind me. I wanted to saver this, but my brain wouldn't slow down.

"Donatus Sun, Donatus Sun, Donatus Sun," my brain wouldn't shut up.

I slid out from under James' arm. I could see his wavy hair in the darkness framing his angular face, full mouth, and cleft chin. In the dark it looked like a Roman man of 20 had stepped out of a mid-century painting and crawled into my bed.

Alpha's tail began thumping after I opened the bedroom door.

"Sssshhhh." I motioned for her to follow me into the living room.

Grabbing my remote off the coffee table I reclined on my couch pulling an afghan over me as Alpha settled on the floor. A low warning growl emanated from her throat. I looked out the front window over the couch; I hadn't bothered to close the venetian blinds. I turned on the TV and muted the sounds. I looked out again and noticed one of the neighbor's floodlights was on, probably a squirrel. The television said it was 3:45 a.m.

I turned the channel to MTV, lucked out, and got the news. After a short piece on Washington's garage band scene I saw a familiar face. I turned up the sound just loud enough to make out each word. Donatus Sun was reclining against a large stage amp and smoking a cigarette. The interview was from a few months ago.

"Throughout its history there have always been good, passionate bands in rock 'n' roll. It's up to fans and the music industry to make sure it doesn't get as bad and as stale as it has within the last ten years."

A slight smile played on his face as he brushed his blond disheveled hair out of his eyes. He wore a black leather jacket, beat up ripped jeans, pummeled sneakers and long johns. If the camera hadn't panned in close to reveal how expensive his jacket was, you'd think a Good Will had thrown up on him. He looked bummy, apathetic, and impossibly cool.

"What are your plans for the future?" asked a disembodied voice off camera. Donatus' eyes squinted in a contemplative study of the inside of his wrist.

"It'd be nice to eventually start playing acoustic and be thought of as a singer-songwriter, rather than just another postmodern rocker, because then I might be able to take advantage of that when I'm older. I could sit in a chair, play acoustic guitar like Leonard Cohen, and it wouldn't be a big joke. Who knows?"

If there was a John Lennon figure for the Postmodern generation, it would be Donatus Sun. Had I not known who he was, I would never have guessed the young man chain-smoking American

Spirits with holes in his jeans was worth millions, possibly a billion dollars in potential royalties.

4

"Brittany."

I opened my eyes to the inside of my couch, and inhaled the scent of dog, gun oil, coco butter, and sunflower conditioner. The upholstery could use cleaning. I rolled over to see my television flickering a music video featuring a busty blonde in a red bikini taking off her sunglasses to reveal reptile eyes. Her tongue snapped out of her mouth to catch a fly. Distorted guitars serenaded her as she gave a psychedelic bleached, capped- tooth smile.

"Are you ok? Why did you sleep on the couch?" James was standing in his boxers, which revealed that other parts of him were also half awake.

"What time is it?"

"Eight AM."

"I'll let Alpha out and come to bed."

"She's fine. I already did." James scooped me up off the couch and carried me into the bedroom.

#

The hotel room had been propped open, so we let

ourselves in. Her bed was made, but she was still wearing the same negligee as yesterday. Her hair was combed a bit, but her makeup had been reapplied so many times her face was a hardened paint palette. I imagined a painter with an easel standing next to her bed swirling his paintbrush around her eyelashes and dipping it onto her lips as she lay there. Did Cherry leave for house cleaning to come in, or did she simply lie there in her underwear as they cleaned around her?

Cherry sucked on her cigarette and exhaled. "I called the credit card company like you said, and they told me Donatus also bought two airlines tickets."

"Where to?" James asked. We took a seat on the couch, moving four red and gold accent pillows out of the way.

"They don't know, or they won't tell me. All they would say was how much he paid for them." Her eyes narrowed as she stared up at the ceiling and puffed away at her cigarette. She sat up and uncrossed her legs to reach for an ashtray on the bedside table. We got more view than we wanted for the third time in two days. The room was cleaned up, but still had that sickening smell I couldn't put my finger on.

"Anyway, I figure he…"

James stood up and handed her a blanket that had been folded on a nearby dresser.

"…he flies up to Seattle, gets his guitar, then flies to his show in Atlanta, but he has two tickets. I mean, did he get it for someone else?"

The same young woman with a shock of red hair entered from the sitting room as Cherry began to cry.

The woman took a seat and Cherry followed her, kneeling beside her on floor cushions. She tried to soothe Cherry by rubbing up and down her arms.

"I think Donatus wants a divorce."

"Why would you say that?" I asked. Something didn't feel right. Why hadn't she asked us if we found anything yet?

"He left me a note when he was in Rome. He said he was leaving me," she sobbed.

"When he had his accident?"

Cherry stared off over my shoulder, either deep in thought or seeing something we couldn't. How many drugs had she taken today? Had she slept?

"If me and Donatus got into a divorce, and it came down to a custody battle... he'd better not the son of a bitch."

Her grammar was as good as her guitar playing.

"The only way a divorce will happen is if I bust him for infidelity."

"Has he been unfaithful?" James eyed Cherry the way one would eye a sedated rabid dog.

"Fuck. Yes, I think so. I know he was having an affair with my bassist, Kristie White. Neither of them will admit it. He might be having an affair with his drug dealer, Jessica. I bet anything it's her he's cheating on me with." Cherry pointed her cigarette at us. "I have people, staff, on the lookout right now."

I could see it in her pinned blue eyes. She was insanely jealous of anybody who got close to Donatus, and she wasn't kidding about wanting to know every little move he made.

"So, I planted a story in the news yesterday saying that I had OD'd, and I was in the hospital thinking that Donatus would get scared and call me. I don't know, like, I got this record coming out in a week. I now know the value of this publicity, and I didn't even think about it when I first called in the report." Cherry's eyes grew big and wild. "All publicity is good publicity, to a certain degree... unless you're Phil Spector."

Cherry made a gun with her thumb and forefinger firing it at her friend. The redhead tittered with laughter. I looked at James who looked back at me with an eyebrow raised. This chick was all over the place.

"Called in what report?" I asked.

"That I OD'd. If it goes in, the rumor, and I deny it, and my fans will believe me if I deny it, that's when the rumor mill starts. I'm an expert at this." Cherry lit up another cigarette and waved it around.

"Then they'll say, "Oh, Donatus left. Cherry got depressed. She had to be hospitalized. What an asshole. If it's not drugs, it must have been a nervous breakdown. Then it appears that I attempted suicide. That way there are no drugs involved, and the sympathy goes to me. How's that for a spin?"

I pulled out my tape recorder and hit record. Cherry shook her head, flapping both her hands down repeatedly to mime, *put that away*, like it was a poisonous spider she wanted put back in its terrarium. James shrugged as I feigned a click on the stop button, and threw the tiny, still recording tape recorder back

31

into my handbag. "Thanks for the heads up. We need to know what's floating out there in the media for us to do our job. Aren't you worried that Donatus will find out you were never really in the hospital?"

"No. No one will tell him."

"How can you be sure?" James asked.

She leaned forward and squinted at James, and spoke extra slow. "The people I had do this, I paid. The press portrays me as tragic anyway. I have a record coming out. This shit sells."

"Cherry, Genevieve's going to be here in half an hour," said the redhead, staring at the floor with her chin in her palm.

"Right. Right. Shit."

"You need to shower up if you're going to talk to the…"

"Yes, I fucking know Tanya. Listen you guys. Can we take lunch and you guys can come back in a couple hours or so?"

I smiled and nodded. Who knew what this was about? What did I care? Cherry would be billed for all of it and I wouldn't have to sweat the company overhead for a few months. "How about we give you three and a half to be safe. See you in a bit."

"Thanks you guys," Cherry said. This time she walked us out and smiled as she shut the door.

Downstairs I handed the ticket to the valet at the podium. "The charge is to Room 226."

"Thank you, ma'am."

I reached in my bag and clicked off my trusty recorder. I tested it. It got damn near everything.

"She's hiding something," said James.

"Of course, she's a celebrity."

The Impala rumbled up beside us.

"What a beautiful car, sir. Have you ever thought about selling it?"

The young man handed James the keys, straightening his vest.

"It belongs to the lady," said James, tossing me the keys.

"Sorry." The kid blushed.

"I get offers all the time. Can't sell it. It's family."

I hit up the first newsstand I saw. The front cover of *Verve Music* magazine was Donatus and Cherry. She kissed his cheek as he smiled a dimpled smile and held her in his arms.

Back at The Flamenco I paged P.I. Tom Depot and he called me back within minutes. No word on Donatus' dealer and possible lover, Jessica Black.

5

From its exterior the restaurant was quaint and without a sign. No advertising indicated it was exclusive, or anything but quaint on the inside. Potted orchids in full bloom on every surface made the space feel like a catered wedding venue.

Once seated at a "handcrafted" wood table that looked like it was purchased from an antique auction house, the tattooed waitress with double Ds flipped her blonde hair, smiled at us, and handed us each a menu.

"This isn't where I imagined perfect flavor and vitamin combinations?" I turned over the menu.

The menu had a headshot and brief bio of every bleached smiled server.

James pointed to a big chested beauty, "She's the one I dated."

"Says on the menu, *Justice teaches yoga and practices transcendental meditation.*"

"Yoga, and moonlighting as a whole grains pusher. During a past life transgression meditation she said she found out she was a race car driver in her past life.

I told her that the probability level wasn't too hot, considering she was born before NASCAR really took off."

"I take it there wasn't a second date?"

James shook his head.

I cracked open *Verve Magazine*, and read the article as James ordered for us. When I tried handing it over he shook his head.

"Already read it."

"For a celebrity who despises the press, Cherry sure gives a lot of interviews." I blew on my Earl Grey tea and stirred in some honey.

"Indulge the lesser powers without increasing their power."

I laughed, "It's a bit rich, but do you think Cherry is pulling a power play from Machiavelli's, *The Prince*?

"Don't you? It's amazing how she can get away with it. A simple well-placed phone call from the right person re-writes history."

Back at the hotel we were greeted by an older, stouter valet who simply sighed when we gave him our room number. Once in the room I was expecting a possible news reporter, only to find a stylishly dressed bespectacled blonde woman in her late forties.

"I'll send them a cease and desist, but Cherry, please, try to lead a tabloid free life until we get this situation resolved."

"Ok. Yes. I told you. I'm agreeing with you."

The woman looked James and me over.

"They're two of my private investigators."

Two of, how many did she have? "Hello, Brittany

Wolfe," I said shaking hands. The blue-eyed blonde had 'better not fuck with me' tattooed on her brow.

"Genevieve Townsend." She handed me a card and Cherry crossed her legs and began fidgeting with her black stocking. I thought she looked familiar. I had seen photos of her next to Cherry and Donatus in a popular magazine. She was their entertainment lawyer. Cherry's eyes locked on her attorney's card in my hand.

"Donatus told me he had Little Chris purchase the shotgun because he had intruders in the house. He thought they were sent from the label..." the lawyer began.

"Genevieve, I'm afraid he's going to hurt himself."

Cherry looked very different from just a few hours ago. Freshly scrubbed, she shined up well, and she was wearing real clothes. Her platinum shoulder length blonde hair had been washed, blow dried, and coiffed.

She wore a short black dress with a white collar that plunged at the neck revealing cleavage like it was meant for a slutty Wednesday Adams. Two small, shiny red plastic barrettes the same color as her full, lipsticked pout were clipped on either side of her head. Black thigh highs clung to her skinny legs, and black patent leather Mary Janes had just enough heel to make her significantly taller.

"When I last spoke to him from the hospital he said he was thinking about taking a break from Bliss. The word must have gotten out. Now, do you know anyone who would have done that?" Genevieve said.

"Can you take them into the sitting room," Cherry turned to the redhead, now with sniffles, who motioned for us to follow her through the French doors. Cherry's eyes were wide and awake. Her lips full and pursed as if their rich hungry fullness were draining the rest of her body of nutrients.

"Nice to meet you," James and I said. Genevieve nodded, and then looked sideways at Cherry. What was Cherry afraid of?

"This is so bizarre." James looked around the sitting room, which appeared like it hadn't been touched. We could see that the cavernous stone bathroom had been used. Damp white towels were everywhere. A mirrored jewelry tray sat conspicuously empty but for some white powdered residue.

We sat in silence for a minute.

"Do you live in LA?" asked James.

"Yeah. I live off Sepulveda," the redhead sniffed.

"Are you from here?" I smiled. Manners cost nothing.

"Nope. Boston." She sniffed again as she lit a cigarette, the smoke instantly masked the room's pine fresh scent. By the time she finished it, the scent of pine had been destroyed.

The three of us jumped as the French doors flung open. Cherry Starlet rested her hands on either side of the frame, as if striking a pose. "I'm ready for you now. This day has been fucking taxing!"

"Is everything OK?" James asked. I pressed my tape recorder's record button down in my purse.

Cherry lit a cigarette and began pacing.

"With Donatus, it's like, 'Yeah, well fuck you – I don't want to even be in Bliss anymore.' Jesus. If Donatus wants to turn his nose up at nine point five million dollars at the biggest music festival of the decade when Toyland could've fucking played the festival, and gotten a cut. We wouldn't have made what he could make, but still."

I knew her story from stuff I'd read before. What I didn't know I filled in a bit with what I'd read in *Verve*. Cherry was the front woman for the band Toyland. Their work consisted mostly of cleavage, bronchial screams, and feminist rants that were almost poignant, until they weren't. Toyland released their first album, *Va-Va-Voom and Violence* and made three million dollars. Months after their first tour they went broke. Later, after dating a handful of rock stars while relentlessly following Bliss, Cherry married Donatus. Toyland was then signed to Bliss' record label and Cherry was finally given guitar lessons.

I noticed a small book that looked like a religious pamphlet near Cherry's elbow. The heading said, *Veritas Society*, with the symbol of an upright pen balancing scales of justice.

"…when I've been able to talk to him and go, Donatus, I love you. I'll support you in whatever you choose to do. Toyland could have done the festival this year, but I made my band give that up so Donatus could go out and make nine million, ten million dollars. And now, he's fucking everything up."

As we watched her pace, her mind spinning I knew there was more we weren't being told. While listening to Cherry rant all done up in her 'blonde aspirations' attire, I could understand what Donatus saw in her. Energy and stamina vibrated off her like a malignant contagion. She was so close to us I could smell her each time she walked by. Her odor was of a cutthroat ambition gone sour. Her long slender legs, big breasts, and threatening stance made her beguilingly masculine.

"Have you two found anything?" asked Cherry.

"Donatus' mother, Brianne Knight, filed a missing persons report. In it she claimed Donatus fled a facility; won't say which one and that she's worried about her son because she believes he's suicidal, and knows he's in possession of a gun. If they're estranged, how would she know any of this?"

I tried to gage Cherry's reaction. Her face was a blank slate. "We're looking into who actually filed the report. My Seattle support should be getting back to us with the info soon." Would she call this off? We really needed the money.

"I called Seattle police and filed the missing persons report. I'm concerned about my husband."

"You filed it?" James uncrossed his legs and gripped his knees. "That's going to cause a hell of a lot of confusion. Why did you use Brianne's name? You could get in a lot of trouble."

"I did it because no one would take me seriously if I filed it under my own name. We needed to get things going, right? Well, I got it going." Cherry sat down on the love seat next to the bed and crossed her legs. Her demeanor was completely different from yesterday.

39

She was awake. Alive. "Have you checked in to Donatus' dealer, Jessica Black? If he's in Seattle they're together."

"I've got someone watching her apartment. Donatus hasn't shown up. I want to put somebody on your house, too, because sooner or later he's going to go home."

"Listen, if Donatus is in Seattle he's hiding out. He's not going to be at the house. He likes to stay at hotels, fancy hotels downtown, like this one." Cherry motioned around the room with her cigarette, leaving a thin trail of blue smoke in the air. "He uses the name Greg Travis, or Simon Webster."

I handed Cherry an itemized bill. She took out her checkbook and scribbled. "Let me know if this will cover you guys for the next few days."

I took the check. It more than covered it.

Down in the lobby I spotted a man who looked like a spook wearing dark sunglasses, a black suit, and carrying a black briefcase. On the briefcase was the same symbol I saw on Cherry's pamphlet, the upright pen balancing scales of justice.

6

It was smooth sailing taking Sepulveda instead of the 405, but now were trapped in bumper-to-bumper hell on the Santa Monica Freeway. Wasn't someone shot while sitting in this last week because they cut off the wrong guy? I eyed my glove box containing my 9mm and magazine I loaded with this morning's fresh clip.

When we finally made it to the office, I slowed down right before the gate. Holding the electric clicker in my hand I stopped the car, but didn't hit the button.

"What are you waiting for? Aren't you ready to be out of the car yet?" James asked.

I pointed at the car across the street. It was closer to us now than it had been when we saw it in the Valley. I saw the same sexless baseball hat sitting in a parked four-door silver sedan wearing the same turtleneck attire. James and I stared for a minute and gave each other a look. The sedan slowly left its parking space and turned left around the corner.

It wasn't unusual to see people waiting in their cars around this residential/commercial neighborhood, but

I didn't believe in coincidences; I was convinced the sedan was tailing us. After parking behind our electric gate, I got out and looked around. The sedan was gone. James shrugged and I followed him inside.

"That's weird."

I checked my messages and Tom Depot had left three. I scribbled all the information down, and then called Cherry.

"We didn't have success with any of the fancy downtown hotels, so we tried calling the smaller ones."

I detected the quick intake of breath on the other line. "Oh, he must be holed up at one of his friend's houses."

"Well, we looked into some motels and were able to locate a Greg Travis registered near the Aurora Strip. We'll send one of our guys over there."

"Brittany, no. I don't want Donatus to know I'm looking for him."

"What? But..."

"Go ahead and send somebody over there, but just have them watch the motel," said Cherry.

"Alright." I hesitated. Why was she upset about this development?

"Thanks. Call me if you find anything else."

The phone went dead.

"I'm going to go check on my bike," James said, putting down a newspaper at his makeshift desk - a TV tray in front of our guest seating.

"OK." I hung up the dead phone.

I tried to wrap my head around how this gig paid more in a week than we normally made in three

months. Cherry was hardly requiring us to lift a finger. Ten minutes went by and the phone rang again.
"Stacks Private Investigators."

"It's not him," Cherry said on the other end.

"Wait. What?"

"I spoke to the man registered and it's not him."

Surprised it was Cherry, I collected my thoughts.

"What do you mean? You called the motel? I thought you said you didn't want Donatus to know?"

"No, Brittany. I just had to talk to him. You don't understand."

I took a breath. She's the client, and she pays. But paying for what? What did she want? "Listen, if he's not at the motel, then we need to set up a team at your lake house in Seattle."

"It's a waste of time, Brittany."

"Is there a particular reason you don't want us surveilling your house?"

"Yes, Little Chris, err, my friend Chris Rome is there. He's the live-in nanny and he'll call me if Donatus shows up."

I'd had enough of this. The money was good, but it had to be hands on or nothing.

"I'd like to move the entire search up to Seattle. I got guys on the ground, local guys. If I were up there I could move things along faster."

"That's fine. You can go."

"That's great. You'll probably want to go up there as well, considering the situation. Where and when should we meet?"

"Brittany, I can't. I have business in LA."

"I'd appreciate it if you didn't tell anyone that I'm going up there. If anyone knows, they might tell Donatus and he could flee."

"Absolutely. I think that's a good idea. Spare no expense and send me the bill. All I want is to find my husband."

I heard the office door open and shut. Sighing, I set down my notepad and hung up the phone.

"James, you aren't gonna believe this."

I heard a sputter and looked up.

"James!"

James' face was covered in blood. He whole body shuddered as he collapsed into his chair.

7

"Tell me what happened. Do you need to go to the hospital? Are they still outside? How many of them are there?"

"Trisha." James said through clenched teeth.

Just one demon whore from hell. "Was she in touch with you again?"

I handed James a towel from the hall closet as he took a seat in front of my desk. His nose was bleeding good, the blood turning the blue towel a deep purple.

"Yes, I told her the only reason I kept answering was I couldn't stand it when she approached me in person. I was trying to be nice. I told her it made me feel bad to see her cry. Then out of nowhere, she runs up and tases me. While I was down she kicked me in the face. When she tried to kick me a second time I grabbed her leg and grounded her." James' face was swelling rapidly.

"I'm calling the cops."

"That won't do anything."

"But, your restraining order..."

"...isn't worth the paper it's printed on. Come on

Brit. You know just as well as I do Trisha waited for me to be alone so it's my word against hers. No witnesses. She can only be arrested if she's caught on the premises."

He was right. She even attacked him in the garage. The one place we don't have cameras.

Trisha Cooke is a beautiful graduate student from Philadelphia about to get her master's in clinical psychology with honors. She was scheduled to enroll in a Ph.D. program at Columbia. She was also still obsessed with her failed relationship with James.

James came from a prominent New Jersey family; Trisha was a rebound after he got back from his first stint in rehab. "I was a recent law school grad, and she was a six-month convenience. To her I was, the one. After I got a job with a reputable firm a co-worker introduced me to Miss Rhode Island. Trisha didn't take it well."

"That's putting it mildly." I tried to keep the sarcasm out of my voice.

"She's an Italian East Coast broad. I pushed her over the edge," James groaned.

I rolled my eyes. Her intense neediness was not his doing. When she got word he had a date lined up with the beauty queen, she broke into his apartment while he was taking a shower, and fired a gun next to his head.

James leaned his head back, removing the towel. "She was screaming about me screwing whores and never appreciating her. When I overpowered and sat on her she cried that this was the only way she could

46

talk to me and try to work things out."

Trisha might be nuttier than a flying squirrel monkey, but she wasn't stupid. If she didn't always plan five steps ahead, she'd be locked up by now. James could go down to the cop shop and have them drag her in for assault, but she'd have some wild story that would put him at fault, and might even get him arrested.

"Don't file a complaint, just a report. You at least need to get it documented."

"Yeah. I think I'm done bleeding."

Too bad James can't pour bourbon on his wounds. My first instinct was to get him a beer, and hell, one for myself. I could have one or two. I had focus pills in my desk somewhere, but I needed to save them for a time of desperation.

"I'll get us some coffee."

"I'll take an Americano. Watch out for Trisha."

"I'll be sure to taze her if I see her," I said giving James a thumbs up. Now that his nose has stopped bleeding it really didn't look that bad.

I walked around the corner to get us two coffees and buy some time. James wasn't going to like me in a minute. The line seemed never ending. What's with all this fancy coffee? Suddenly coffee out of the communal work pot didn't work for people anymore. I came back with two venti Americanos.

"Oh, thanks. I need this. How's my face look?"

"Not bad. Your nose is a little swollen, but at least it's not broken."

"Yeah, I'm lucky she was wearing her sensible

47

shoes."

"I just spoke to Cherry on the phone. I asked if I could move the entire search up to Seattle, and she agreed to it."

"Great. When do we leave?"

"We don't. I'm rolling solo on this one." I promised Cherry extra coverage, and she was going to get it, but not from James.

His mouth opened in disbelief. I tried to look away.

"Solo? Why can't I come with? You *need* me. You can't just poke around in the Seattle underworld, you know, alone."

He meant alone as a woman. My 9mm had a faster response time then James' fist, but I wasn't going to point that out. Men like to feel needed.

"I know James. I prefer you over Tom any day."

"You'll be working with Tom? He's your get away plan? What the fuck can that chain smoking booze sponge get away from? I'd pay to see him run one mile without having a cardiac arrest."

"James, look at it this way. You haven't been in recovery all that long."

James opened his mouth to protest.

"I have to bounce around drug dealers to find this guy. What would Joe say when he found out where you were?"

James closed his mouth and looked at his hands. He knew I was right.

"I'll have Anne Marie house sit for me, and I'll try not to be gone more than a few days."

James nodded. Was he scared to be alone? Next to

working out, I was his best distraction.

"You want to spend the night tonight?"

"Sure."

8

It was raining hard when I landed at Sea-Tac
Airport. I wore black-heeled boots, a green rain jacket,
and carried a large black umbrella. By the time I got to
the car rental place I was drenched, despite my attire.

After picking out a black Honda Accord, I missed
my Impala as I drove to the diner where Cherry
wanted me to meet with Donatus' best friend, Synroc
Landall.

Seated at the diner, a cup of coffee and a bowl of
bread pudding in front of him, the man with blue eyes
and a dark flannel jacket spotted me right away. He
stood up as I approached his old Formica table. The
dingy little place was clearly built in the '50s,
renovated in the '70s, then left to pot. The coffee, bread
pudding, even the short stacks of pancakes being
served by frowny-faced waitresses all had a weird
greyish quality to them.

"Hi, you must be Brittany." The man smiled not
unattractively. He shook my hand. "I'm Synroc."

"Nice to me you," I said taking a seat. "I'm told
you're Donatus' best friend."

"Have been for almost ten years. He even had my band open for Bliss up until the record label took over complete control. He's so over that label."

It was starting to click. An anti-hero like Donatus was the only voice that could ever be accepted by a generation that purposefully defied the commercialization of its experience. As soon as they felt something aimed at them as target market, the Postmodern Generation dodged it. Or maybe I'd taken too many uppers on the plane.

"It's Cherry's label now as well, right?"

"Yeah, Cherry and Toyland. Their new album's actually pretty good, although you can tell what musicians are behind the songs."

"Are you saying Cherry doesn't write her own stuff?"

Synroc gave a noncommittal shrug.

"So, what do you think about all this?" The menu had onion-loaded cheesy chili fries as its special. I shuddered. "Do you think Donatus is suicidal?"

"No, not at all." Synroc crossed his arms and shook his head. "He's been under a lot of pressure, but he's been handling things pretty good. He and Cherry have been having a lot of troubles lately. I don't know why he married her. They don't get along. They don't agree on anything. They're always fighting."

"What did they last fight about?"

"Oh, shit. They fight so much, I don't even remember. Oh, yeah. Cherry bought herself a rose gold Mercedes with white leather, and they have a two-year-old! Donatus made her take it back. In fact, he left and wouldn't come back to the house until she did. Man, did that piss her off. She never did fully let that one go."

"This thing that just happened in Rome, did anyone say that was a suicide attempt?"

"No, it was an accident. Everybody knows that. Rohypnol is a touchy drug. Donatus does it when he's trying not to do heroin. Wait, is that what Cherry's saying?"

I tried to crack a smile, "It's strange, right? I'm thinking, if you thought Donatus was trying to kill himself, like Cherry claims he was, why would you let him buy a shotgun?"

"He's not suicidal. I bought the shotgun for him the day before he went to rehab. There had been a break in. Donatus was paranoid it had to do with his label and manager. I don't know why he had his promoter managing him. Your promoter's main objective is to get you out on the road. Donatus was convinced he was being threatened. It had something to do with his last minute pull out of the touring festival Bliss was headlined to do. It's going to cost the label and his management team millions."

"Why did you have to buy the shotgun? Why didn't he just buy it himself?"

"He and Cherry had gotten into a domestic dispute. The cops showed and separated them. The cops asked Donatus if he had any guns in the house, he said no. When they asked Cherry, she said yes. They seized his whole collection, all 14 firearms. Because the police had just confiscated his guns I had to register the shotgun in my name."

"Why does Cherry keep saying Donatus is suicidal?"

"Because she wants help finding him. Power and control, I don't know. Trust me, if I thought he was suicidal I would never have let him get a shotgun."

So, Donatus was paranoid that record executives were out to get him for screwing with their financial trajectory. So far, that was the first thing to make sense during this whole investigation. Donatus wasn't necessarily hiding out from Cherry, but from whom?

"Are you ready to take me to the lake house?"

"I have to call Cherry first. Wait here. There's a payphone outside."

I got the feeling Cherry would be quarterbacking this entire process. Rain pelted the restaurant windows hard. I could make out Synroc's profile at the phone booth.

I pulled out my notepad. On it I traced over the names Greg Travis and Simon Webster. Next to it was the note –*check fine hotels downtown*. Synroc resumed his seat across from me. He sipped his coffee and ate some more of his bread pudding. A true junkie meal. Junkies like sweets. Synroc's short clipped hair was lined with little sores. His skin was dry with a greenish tinge; evidence of a long-standing habit. It must have been hard living in Donatus' shadow.

"My electronica grunge band has a new LP coming out. It's featuring a lot of real strings - violin, stand-up bass, and viola. It should be pretty sick." Synroc smiled, but his eyes weren't into it. The light had gone out of his soul a long time ago. That's what addiction does. I'd tried to get to the man's core, but I don't think he has one.

The sky was black as we drove through the pouring rain, past manicured hedges and through a gate. I could tell we were on private property. Driving around a large fountain of a naked female with angel wings, I pulled in front of the mansion's cavernous entrance. Stopping, I took in the view through the rain.

"I'll go knock on the door and see if anyone's home," Synroc said as he climbed out of my car.

The rain let up briefly, just long enough for me to take in the three-story mansion. The early 18th century New England style home's exterior consisted of weathered dark wood shingles with white frosted windows and balconies to outline its details. Flanked by wet English gardens and manicured lawns, the place had a cozy, peaceful feel. I was having a hard time envisioning Donatus living here. Wouldn't he see this as being a traitor to his audience? I thought back to something he said in a music journal.

Art that has long lasting value cannot be appreciated by majorities. Only the same, small percent will value art's patience as they always have. We need to stay humble, and sidestep the stagnation created by trappings of success as much as possible.

As the rain picked up again, the passenger door of my rental opened and shut. Synroc had poured himself back into the passenger seat wet and shivering.

"Anything?"

"No." Synroc crossed his arms, his hands in the armpits of his damp flannel jacket.

"Are you sure he's not in there?"

"I knocked for at least five minutes. If he's there he would have answered."

"Alright. I just don't want to end up on the wrong end of a shotgun." I tried to gage Synroc's comfort level as he unfolded his arms and stared at his hands. Water from his hair dripped onto his jeans. This was probably the cleanest that flannel jacket had been in a while. He smelled like wet camping gear.

"You know how to get in?"

"Yeah, a couple of ways. I know the code to the alarm. We'll have two minutes to turn it off."

"Let's go," I said opening my car door.

I followed Synroc over to the side of the house, to a window between two hedges. Synroc pushed open the window. It yielded without much effort.

"That's strange."

"What?"

"The alarm's not on. It's never not on. Little Chris always remembers to set it. Whoa. This place is a lot cleaner than it usually is."

"Synroc," I said through the window. "Make lots of noise. Call out, *Donatus!* Stomp. Make noise so we don't scare anyone."

"Ok. Donatus? Donatus!"

I climbed in after him. Synroc began turning on industrial metal and glass standing lamps to light up our way. I followed him through the living room, and up the three-level staircase.

As we began to climb, Synroc pointed to a doorway at the bottom of the staircase. "That's where Little Chris and his girlfriend stay. Little Chris used to date Cherry, now Cherry has them keep to their room because they're "staff." If Donatus is here without her they use the whole house. He really hates that Cherry pushes them around, and I'm like, Donatus, she pushes you around, too."

"Where are Little Chris and his girlfriend now?"

"Who knows. They're definitely not here. The place is too clean."

That depends on your definition of clean. There were empty bags of potato chips and coke cans scattered here and there. There were fresh looking cigarette butts and ash in the ashtrays. It was far from immaculate. It simply looked like the house had been vacuumed, swept, and the counters wiped up. On the second floor we passed a child's room and a guest room. Two French doors led to a master bedroom with an attached bath. I followed Synroc inside.

"She has that closet over there dedicated to just lingerie. Cherry always blows money in a big way. You could take some. The tags are still on. I bet they'd look foxy on you."

I laughed, assuming he was joking. Then I studied him more carefully. He was serious. Hope springs eternal in the drug addled mind.

"Let's check the guest room. If Donatus came home and he's mad at Cherry like you said, he might not have slept in here."

"Sure." Synroc shrugged.

We walked into the open guest room. The pristine duvet cover and pillows on the bed were as untouched as the master bedroom. I made my way toward the closet. If I could find the shotgun, and get it out of the house, I'd at least have accomplished something. I opened the doors and jumped back.

"Holy shit!"

"What is it?" asked Synroc.

Two tall figures in the closet stared down on me. Were they dead? I couldn't see any ropes. Synroc hurried over to my side. He reached out and pulled a cord. Light switched on from above. We stared at two statues of biological anatomy models made of fiberglass. Both were females, complete with intestines, uterus, and heart. Their left arms were fleshless muscle, their right arms bone.

"Ha! They're from the *Gray's Anatomy* world tour."

"*Gray's Anatomy*, that was Bliss' last album, right? The featured single was, *Heart Shaped Cage*." I remembered James talking about it as he insisted I listen to his disks.

Synroc looked impressed. "Did you like it?"

"It was interesting. A bit different from Bliss' others. I have a friend from New Jersey who's a diehard fan." I had mixed feelings about the distorted sound from the album, *Gray's Anatomy*. Yet, there was no denying Donatus' creative genius. Even when he was trying to isolate himself from more fans and stardom, the muse kept coming; it was like he couldn't help himself.

"Let's check the master bedroom again for the gun, then we can get out of here."

I followed Synroc across the hall. He dropped to his knees at the California king size bed centered across from a wall of windows and looked under it, while I checked the closets.

"So, the mainstream media found him. Donatus is the most unlikely American icon in history," I said, looking around the room in awe that anyone could achieve that much success accidentally.

"Donatus wanted mainstream success. You don't get here without an element of planning. He perpetuates this myth that he was swept up into this media frenzy, but everything he did was to get more famous. Then Cherry came into the picture and it exploded. Now he hates the press and wishes he could go back to playing small clubs and lounges. It's punk alienation packaged as marketable mainstream pop," Synroc said.

He was certainly speaking freely about what he thought of Donatus in the man's own house. He wasn't worried he could be overheard by his best friend right now? I opened another closet wary of more life-sized statues. "Both these closets had only women's clothes and shoes."

"Yeah, Donatus only uses drawers. Cherry probably gave him one in here," Synroc said. "She always complains about how small this place is, for a five-bedroom manor with a third floor," Synroc laughed.

I joined him at the bed and began taking off the pillows. We heaved and pushed off the top mattress. Synroc picked up a plastic Ziploc bag filled with pills.

"Rohypnol. That's where they were! He kept saying someone stole them, but they were here the entire time." Synroc rolled up the bag and stuffed it in his back pocket. "Cherry's cool if I keep these. They're prescription, from England. They're a sedative for sleeping ailments and such."

"Synroc."

"Yeah?"

"Is there anywhere else we should look?"

#

Back at my motel I checked in with James. Tired, I quickly debriefed him.

"Have you heard anything from Cherry?" I asked.

"No, but I've been filling my time with research. Cherry has multiple restraining orders against her. She's punched out journalists and photographers. She's sent death threats to biographers. Her attorney must make a fortune off her."

"That's interesting. I'll keep that in mind," I said. "Still no sign of the shotgun. I don't even know what I'm doing up here." Actually, I did. I was trying to save our LA office from shutting down.

"Just be careful, Brittany."

James almost always called me Brit. Suddenly, I felt very far away.

9

I refused to acknowledge the ringing for as long as I could. Pulling the pillow over my head I tried to block it from my ears. It penetrated the cloth incessantly. I picked up the phone and immediately slammed it back down on its cradle. What the fuck time was it? I didn't ask for a wake-up call. Did this dump even offer that kind of service? I could hear the rain pelting against my little motel window. Single pane. Staying in a dive to save a buck seemed like a good idea last night.

The phone rang again. I picked it up, tempted to throw it across the room.

"What?!"

"I need you and Synroc to go back to the house again. I just... I forgot to tell you to look for other stuff."

"What? Cherry, what other stuff?"

"Just meet Synroc at the same café in like three hours. Okay?" Click.

God damn crazy lady.

Synroc was at the same booth we sat in yesterday. I ordered coffee, eggs, and toast.

"Cherry wants us to check out their summer cabins up north," Synroc said.

"Sounds good. Should I have my guys check the upscale hotels downtown again?"

"Upscale hotels?" Synroc played with his coffee cake.

"Yeah, Cherry said that Donatus likes to stay in the best hotels."

Synroc looked up from his plate and laughed. "She's so consistent!"

"What do you mean?"

"She's ridiculous. She plays up this rock star bullshit so much. Cherry's a phony. But she's a real phone, because she actually believes all this phony media spin she puts out and perpetuates. Donatus hates fancy hotels. He stays in really cheap places, mostly along the Aurora strip. We used to get a room for two to three weeks and basically live off of Coca-Cola and potato chips and do heroin. Then we'd kick. Each time we'd say was our last."

"How often did you do that with him?"

"More than I should have. I need to call Cherry and check in."

"Can I talk to her?"

"She said she prefers to go through me for now," Synroc said.

The waitress brought our food.

"I keep wondering, why Seattle? Why did the postmodern rock scene explode up here? Why not LA, or San Francisco?"

Synroc smiled a little as he looked up at me, then

back at his plate. "Seattle has always had this sense of isolation. Before this millionaire shit happened, you were free to do anything. It's a place where you can be left alone, it's also a place where there's not an expectation you'll succeed. Before all these millionaires landed you were free to try anything. There were no consequences to investing your time in a band. If you failed you'd get another dumb job and put out another record. I mean, what the hell? It's still more than most get done. You could do that here."

I scribbled on a note pad all the places we needed to hit while Synroc went outside to use the payphone. When he came back his brows were knit together.

"Cherry's had some trouble. She was in the hospital, then she was arrested."

"What?"

"She said it was all a big mistake and she's fine. Cops showed up at her room over a disturbance and found a bag of incense believing it was heroin. Genevieve, Donatus' and Cherry's attorney got her out on $2,000 bail."

"Two thousand? For a bag of incense?"

"She probably attacked another reporter," Synroc said.

"Attacked? What do you mean?"

"She's punched people out, broken bottles over their heads, thrown appliances, guitars. It's Cherry." Synroc shrugged. "When that one magazine published that story about her doing heroin while pregnant, she threated the journalist's family, including the dog. I don't think she'd hurt the dog. She just wanted them to know the information she had on them."

"Ready to go to the cabins?" I asked.

"Cherry wants us to go back to the house and look for the shotgun again. She thinks it might be in the hidden compartment of the bedroom closet."

"Hidden compartment?"

"She said that's where he keeps the gun," Synroc said.

Why hadn't she mentioned that before? "Is there any way we can get a house key this time?"

"We'll just go through the window again. I doubt anything's changed."

Once through the window, Synroc was right. The place looked the same. Same ashtrays. Same scattered art work. Nothing looked touched.

"Let's go," I said to Synroc who had gone in the kitchen to check the fridge. On the stairs, between the first and second floor were two pieces of computer paper.

"These weren't there yesterday."

"No." Synroc shook his head. "I'd have seen them."

I picked them up and read them out loud.

-Donatus,

I can't believe you managed to be in this house without me noticing. You are a fucking asshole for not calling Cherry and at least letting her know that you're OK. She's in a lot of pain, Donatus, and this morning she had another accident. She's in the hospital again. She's your wife. She loves you, and you have a child together. Get it together to at least tell her you're OK, or she is going to die. It's not

fair man. Do something now.
  -Lil' Chris

"Synroc, are you sure Donatus isn't depressed?"

"No. Look, I've known him for years. Dark, absolutely. Depressed, fuck no. I've lived with the man. I'd leave our digs, and when I'd come back each time there would be another painting on the wall or he'd have written a song. He's a ball of creative energy; to the point of being unapologetically brave and optimistic. Bliss gets fan mail saying stuff like, I used to beat up homos and I don't anymore because Donatus told me not to. It's insane. He truly is a spokesperson."

I took the papers into the little office area at the bottom of the stairs next to Little Chris' bedroom. The fax machine had a copier. After I had them duplicated I rejoined Synroc on the stairs and put the papers back where I found them. I didn't have much doubt that Little Chris had written the note, but it still looked strange to me. The letter didn't make sense. It looked phony, like a red herring thrown in a piss-poor attempt to hide the obvious.

The rain hadn't let up. Lightning struck three times as we combed over the house and the garage. The two old Volvos hadn't been moved. I could see how Cherry's Mercedes would clash in there. The green sedan and blue station wagon looked like a soccer mom's cars. Neither was the chariot for the queen of rock 'n' roll.

We started on our way to Carnation to see if

Donatus was at the cabins, a "his and hers" kind of deal. After half an hour of driving I stopped for gas. Synroc went to the payphone, then walked back to the car slowly, his hands in his pockets.

"I'm heading inside for a soda," I said putting the gas nozzle away. "You want anything?"

"I just got off the phone with a friend. He said a body was found at the Lake Washington house."

"What?"

I entered the driver's side of the rental and turned on the stereo. *"Donatus Sun's body was discovered today at his Lake Washington House in Seattle. His fans, friends and family mourn his loss."* Seated in the car next to me, Synroc's face was devoid of any emotion.

I fiddled with the stereo on our way back to the lake house. Halfway through the station jumps we hit pay dirt. *"The identity has been confirmed. The body of Donatus Sun, front man for Bliss, was discovered today in the greenhouse of his lake front property by an electrician."*

"The greenhouse? What greenhouse?" I looked at Synroc. His eyes were wide and fearful.

"It's a room above the garage."

"Why didn't we look there?" It was hard keeping the anger out of my voice.

"It's just a dirty little room where they keep firewood and stuff." Synroc looked and sounded tired, as if he had aged 10 years in the last 20 minutes. I could tell he wished to be anywhere but in the car with me.

"How was he there without us knowing? Was he hiding?"

Synroc looked away from me, and sighed. No tears welled up, but his face was pale and drawn.

I searched the stereo slowly turning the dial from left to right until I picked up on some reportage.

A monotone female voice said Bliss and I stopped. *"Bliss front man, Donatus Sun was found dead today of an apparent suicide. The troubled rock star had recently escaped a rehab facility and had been going through some hard times..."*

"Where are they getting all this?" I asked. "Who's giving them that information?"

"It's the press. They're fucking vultures. Donatus hated them." I thought I heard Synroc's voice crack. I was observing a tired and broken man.

I stopped by a payphone on the way back to Seattle.

"James. Have you heard?"

"Yes. Donatus is dead. It's breaking news everywhere. How are you?"

"Fucking pissed, I was just at the house." I debriefed him on the search. "This all feels really wrong. The whole time Synroc has been checking in with Cherry. You got anything?"

"Donatus' credit card company was able to tell me someone had continued using his credit card up until this morning. Is there a time of death yet?"

"Not that I know of. I'm on my way to the crime scene now." I don't know how the hell anyone can announce this as a suicide when there's not even a coroner's report, accept that it's big news. Every reporter wants to have the breaking story."

"Call me after."

"Will do."

"Be careful, and watch what you say to that Synroc guy. Why is he contacting Cherry if he's Donatus' friend? Evidence has a way of disappearing when people smell trouble. How does he support himself in Seattle with a garage band and a heroin habit?"

That was a good question. Cherry was going to be furious with us for not finding her husband fast enough. We should have gotten here a day earlier. We let his life slip through our fingers.

The letter from Little Chris on the stairs; something felt off. The rain had slowed down to a drizzle and the sky was starting to clear as we reached Seattle's Madrona neighborhood. In broad daylight the green house stood out like a spotlighted Hollywood event. You could see it from the street it was so tall, the windows reflected as if electrified; the triangle of windows that made up the roof refracted the sun in a dozen prisms. It was an impressively large greenhouse just begging to be searched. My heart sank. I'd really blown it. Synroc had made it sound like some sort of broom closet.

A policeman stopped us at the entrance. I could make out the bright yellow crime scene tape around the garage and the bushes below the greenhouse over his shoulder.

"You have to be a resident or family to come in here," said the young man who couldn't have been more than 25. "Media stays behind the tape."

"I'm a resident," Synroc said.

"I'll need to see some ID" The cop's peach fuzz

mustache stated fresh out of the academy.

"I was hired by Cherry Starlet," I said pulling out my P.I. badge.

The policeman's mouth opened a bit, and his eyes squinted. "Who?"

"Cherry Starlet's the homeowner and Donatus Sun's wife, or she was," I said.

The uniformed young man knitted his eyebrows together and paused, then nodded and we drove through. The grounds were crawling with media. Men and women with boom mics, cameras, and microphones were literally stumbling up the grassy knolls of the estate as they jockeyed for position.

"Donatus would have absolutely fucking hated this." Synroc looked out his window in disgust. I pulled over and parked near the uncovered part of the garage. Once we exited we made our way toward the front of the house.

"Avoid that guy. He's *Rolling Stone*. They're *Current Affair*, stay away from them," Synroc said pointing. Cameras flashed causing Synroc to spin around. "Fuck off. Fuck off! Have some respect you fucking vultures."

As cameras flashed and people in pantsuits with haircuts inspired by a TV show about friends in New York carrying mics and video cameras chased us in hot pursuit I found what I was looking for. Approaching what looked like the main guys in blue I made eye contact with the man blocking the entrance.

"I'm Brittany Wolfe, how are you?"

"We're not speaking to the press right now. You'll

have to step back behind the line."

"I was hired by Cherry Starlet to investigate the disappearance of her husband. I was in the house today and the night before. I have information that I think would be helpful. Can I please speak to the detective in charge?"

"Wait here," said a Nazi-looking body builder in a cop uniform.

I watched as the muscled cop with light blue eyes and shaved head walked a few feet over to the porch. An older man in uniform with the same shaved scalp sporting a dark grey mustache regarded me through dirty-grey eyes. He had a thin-lipped mouth that twisted like a scar on his square-shaped head. The scar split open revealing some tiny straight, white teeth. What the Nazi was saying seemed to amuse the scar-mouthed detective. The first bald guy came back.

"He says he's too busy to speak to you now. Call the station after 5 p.m. You can talk with him then."

Dumbfounded, I looked from him to the Nazi detective on the porch. That would have never happened in LA, or any other major city for that matter. If I had been investigating a dead body and someone told me they had somebody outside who had been at the crime scene the night before and day of, I'd tell them to hold them; if they said they needed to leave I'd have handcuffed them and kept them there until we could talk to them. It was my opinion that Seattle PD didn't look into anything.

I could tell by the judgmental and cynical air of the investigating parties that this was being treated like a suicide without any additional investigation. If Sgt. Dick McBlueForce was investigating this as a possible homicide he certainly wouldn't have let somebody leave when they'd been in the house the night before and the day of finding a dead body on the property.

Reporters all around us, the buzz of media filled my ears.

"Donatus Sun..." said the voice of one reporter.

"Was found today..." said the voice of another

"... of an apparent gunshot wound to the head," said a high-pitched voice into a microphone.

"His mother filed a missing persons report stating that Donatus was suicidal," said a young man.

I had tape of Cherry admitting to having called in the missing persons report pretending to be Sun's mother. There wasn't even an autopsy report. The media was getting this wrong.

10

Back at another slightly nicer hotel because it listed cable as a feature I set my stuff down and turned on the television and the radio. The cacophony of Donatus Sun reports was deafening.

Music Television news - *"The body of Bliss leader, Donatus Sun, was found in a house in Seattle this morning, dead of an apparently self-inflicted shotgun blast to the head."*

The radio – *"A suicide note was found."*

Music Television news – *"It first got reported by mother Brianne Knight that Donatus Sun was missing. He had fled from a facility and bought a shotgun."*

Cherry was blatantly lying. She had to know I'd be listening to this. She admitted to me she filed the missing persons report. "Wife Cherry Starlet hired private investigator Brittany Wolfe."

You've got to be fucking kidding me. I sat in stunned silence. This was the first time I'd ever heard of a celebrity name-dropping their private detective.

The radio – *"An electrician hired to work on Sun's home made the shocking discovery early-evening, despite the fact Starlet's private investigator, Brittany Wolfe, had already been to the house earlier today."*

Music Television news – *"Unfortunately, the private detective Starlet hired, Brittany Wolfe, failed to find Donatus Sun in time."*

I picked up the phone. James picked up after a few rings. "Hi," I sighed.

"Brittany, Cherry's been calling non-stop. Are you watching the news? She wants you to call her so she can instruct you on how to talk to the press. Genevieve Townsend, her entertainment lawyer also called. She said to call her before calling Cherry."

I was sure Cherry and her famous temper were both going to be venomous when we reconnected. I imagined how Cherry's famous screaming would begin … "You fucking incompetent! I'm going to sue the fuck out of you, then I'll hunt you down and go after your license!" - or worse - "If you think I'm paying you a dime for this you're fucking insane!"

I shuddered.

MTV news – *"On April 4th Donatus Sun's mother, Brianne Knight, filed a missing persons report on her son because he fled a quote, facility. She did not clarify whether it was a treatment center, but that's what people are speculating. She was worried about Donatus because he had a shotgun in his possession, and she considered him suicidal."*

Everything Cherry had already suggested wasn't true was being taken as sacred writ.

"It's said that rocker Cherry Starlet, was in the hospital for anxiety right before Donatus' body was found."

Another lie.

"Her fans are showing their deepest sympathy by gathering in a Seattle park near her residence at this time."

Fishing through my briefcase my fingers clasped on a few sheets of paper, then finally the thick, embossed cardboard of an expensive business card. I dialed the 310 area code.

"Townsend and Lynch."

"Genevieve Townsend, please."

"May I ask who's calling?"

"Private Investigator Wolfe, Cherry Starlet's P.I..."

I was switched over ASAP. The phone began to ring.

"Townsend."

"Hello, Ms. Townsend. This is Brittany Wolfe. I got your message. How are you?"

"Hello. I've been waiting for you to call. We met briefly at the Peninsula Hotel. I've been hearing your voice and seeing your face on the news. I spoke with your partner."

"Yes, that's why I'm calling. I called you before Cherry. You are a partner at this firm?"

"This firm consists of my husband and me. Cherry Starlet and the late Donatus Sun are two of our five clients; Cherry wants you to meet with the Associated Press."

"Yes, and with all due respect, as Cherry's hired P.I. I feel obligated to inform you that I find the circumstances surrounding Donatus Sun's death very suspicious and the information being given to the press to be intentionally inaccurate and cleverly misleading."

I waited for the combat to start.

"I agree."

"I'm sorry?" Did I hear her correctly?

"It's interesting you've not talked to the press. Any of Cherry's other hired P.I.s would have. It's curious. I've done a background check on you, and you're clean. Dig into the past of most P.I.s and you uncover a lot of skeletons. "When do you think you'll be back in LA?"

"I plan to fly back tomorrow morning. I have a meeting to speak with Sgt. McNeil at Seattle PD tonight," I said.

Genevieve cleared her throat and shuffled some papers. "Then can you meet me at my office tomorrow at three? I have some information I'd like to discuss with you off the record, before you speak to the press."

"I'm happy to meet with you, and I have no intention of speaking with the press," I assured her.

"Good. I'll see you then."

"See you soon. Bye."

I called James back.

"How did Cherry sound? Was she raising holy hell for not finding him? Is she blaming us for his suicide? Are we fired?"

"No, not really. She sounded spacy and raspy, like always. She was most concerned about you speaking to the press. Cherry wants the world to know she did everything she could, especially that she hired you to find Donatus. She's been giving phone interviews from her mourning bed. God knows what she's taking.

"I tracked down the photographer who took Bliss' first album cover photos. Her name's Tanya Case. She'll be taking photos of the show that's playing at Raven Lounge in a few hours. According to some reports she and Donatus were good friends."

"Thank you, James. You're amazing."

"You want me to come up there?" He asked, hurried and pushy.

"No. I'll be on the next flight tomorrow."

"Good."

I smiled. "I've got to go."

Pulling up in my Honda rental, I noted that the Seattle Police Department looked very different from the art deco building I worked in for LAPD. The non-organic brick, metal, and glass building stood in stark contrast to its thriving green grass, trees, and the vines running up and down its front and sides. Inside it looked and felt the same. To my complete non-surprise Sgt. McNeil was 45 minutes late for our appointment. Some things never change.

"You were working a missing persons case, right? Hired to find Donatus. Sounds like your job is done. Why did you want to meet with me?" Sgt. McNeil spun a bit in his chair as I crossed my legs and cleared my throat.

"My agency has found numerous inconsistencies. For one, the missing credit card we were strangely hired to track by Cherry Starlet was in continued use through this morning."

"There's any number of reasons that could happen. It doesn't point to murder," said the talking scar. There was resentment in his voice. His thin lips pursed, appearing even thinner, they were no longer under the curtain of his salt and pepper mustache.

"Can I see the crime scene photos?" I wasn't giving up.

"The film hasn't been developed, probably never will be," said the scar.

"May I ask why?"

"We don't develop photographs of suicides."

"Oh! Well, that settles it. It's nice to know you haven't predetermined the case. I would hate to think the media could possibly taint your investigation." I was broke, on the edge of losing a client, and completely sure something was wrong with the suicide angle. I wasn't going to stop asking hard questions. They needed to investigate this as a possible homicide.

"Look, as the lead investigator on this case I assure you, nothing you or anyone else has presented me so far tells me this is anything but a suicide. Now, do you have any more pearls for me?"

"Not at this time." I got up to leave.

Parking wasn't hard to find across the street. I left my 9mm in the center console of the Honda. Raven Lounge was a dark, concrete square centered in the middle of an industrial block. Its stone was painted black and littered with old and new posters and flyers. Randomly adhered stickers of band and skater logos peeled at the edges. The logo of an upright pen balancing scales of justice was painted on one of the exterior walls. Hastily spray painted over it was the

Bliss band logo. When I pulled the heavy door open I was greeted by a bouncer seated in a corner. I handed him my ID and $10 as the noise blasted my ears.

On a stage at the rear of the room young men in t-shirts, jeans, and flannels maltreated two guitars, a bass, and a set of drums. Floor pedals flooded their amps with distortion, as whammy bars were thrust up and down like they were jacking-off their instruments. The drummer hit everything at once as the electric instruments cannibalized themselves, spitting the chrome chunks out in rapid fire. No band name was painted on the masochist's drum set. No flyers indicated who the boys were. As I ordered a beer from the bar I spotted a woman at the stage sporting a camera, big tits, red lips and Bettie Page haircut. I could always spot the type. Beautiful, artistic, well connected and poised. She was going to give me attitude.

I approached the stage. "Tanya Case?"

"Yeah. Who wants to know?"

"My name is Brittany Wolfe. I was hired by Cherry Starlet to find Donatus Sun."

Tanya's blue eyes narrowed. Her brow furrowed, briefly obstructing the alabaster texture of her skin. Apex-level hatred flashed in the blue waters of Tanya's eyes, then disappeared like a pod of orca fins.

"Another one of Cherry Starlet's private Gestapo? I haven't seen him."

"It'd be funny if you had. His body was found at his Lake Washington estate today."

Everything cold and hard in her profile crumbled

away as tears began to fall from her eyes; a statue became human.

"How?"

"We don't know yet. Come sit down. I'll buy you a beer."

At the bar, a surly bleached blonde in a wife beater, bedecked with chest tattoos and metal in her face handed me a cold bottle as I held out another $5. Tanya's head was down, her shoulders shaking. I politely handed over her beer and looked away. After a few minutes, she stopped crying long enough to take a little gold and red porcelain pillbox out of her camera case and pop a few tic-tac-sized yellow ovals before chugging down the beer.

"There was a suicide note," I said before taking a sip of beer. "He had bought a shotgun, and after he escaped from rehab, he was found dead of a shotgun wound to the head."

Tanya sniffed, coughed and breathed a heavy sigh. "Donatus wasn't suicidal. He had Synroc buy that shotgun because he was pulling out of that big festival tour. He said there was a break in earlier and he thought his management and the label could be involved."

"Do you believe that?"

Tanya sniffled and shrugged. "It was hard to tell what was paranoia, you know, because of the drugs he'd been taking."

"And you're sure Donatus wasn't suicidal?"

Tanya nodded. "He's been under a lot of pressure, but no." She shook her head. "He definitely wouldn't have committed suicide."

"Well, that's what Cherry has been feeding the press."

Tanya sneered.

"You two don't get along?"

"Cherry only knew Donatus for six months before they were married. They've only been married for two years and have a two-year-old. She's successful, but she stepped on a lot of people to get where she is. Specifically, Donatus. She has lawyers who are real briefcase bullies."

"I've heard she has a love-hate relationship with the media."

Tanya lit a cigarette and rolled her eyes as she exhaled with a feminine blow. Her bright red lips left a bright red print on the tip of her cigarette.

"She wants me to speak to the media. She's been telling everyone how suicidal Donatus was; that he'd always been that way." I said.

"Cherry has punched out reporters. She's punched out videographers - friends of mine. After a book was published in London on Bliss, Cherry sent private investigators to talk to all Donatus' friends, like 50 of us. She spent quite a bit of money to inquire on who leaked information for the unofficial biography. It was a thinly veiled threat not to talk to the press. When Donatus found out he was furious.

"Stressed yes, but he wasn't suicidal. I can send you interviews with him proving he wasn't. This is all very confusing." Tanya's shoulders slumped as she sobbed and shook. I reached out to pat her back, then thought better of it, stood up, and walked away.

The rain picked up again as I drove back toward Lake Washington. The camping gear smell left over from Synroc in the passenger seat grew stronger as the rain pounded on the roof and windshield. After I entered the open gate I drove past the flourishing, rain soaked hedges and around the circular drive to the front of the house. It was raining so hard I could only see the outline of the stone angel hovering above the center fountain. The yellow outline of crime scene tape still circled the garage.

As I got out of my car, Tom Depot walked out from around the corner of the house.

"Hey, Tom. Staying dry?"

Tom had on a Seattle Seahawks ball cap, black slicker, tennis shoes, and jeans. A damp cigarette dangled from his bulbous lips. The slicker over his rotund body gave him the appearance of a stuffed Hefty bag with a head and feet.

"The only people inside are Cherry, one of her band members, Kate, and Kate's husband. I've been here since 6 a.m. No one else has come or gone. The only lingerers are the reporters on the street. My opinion is that this really was a suicide," said Tom as he chewed on the end of his soggy cigarette.

Cherry had every right to be upset with me. I'd been to the house twice and failed to find Donatus, who could have been in the greenhouse the entire time. Synroc and I could've stopped him.

"Thanks, Tom."

"And Brittany..."

"Yes, Tom?"

"I should warn you. I overheard Cherry yelling on the phone that the detectives she hired couldn't find their ass with both hands, and how she would make sure they paid big time."

Shit. I could envision the only thing I have left of my father being driven away by repo men. I sighed, "I'm Miss World."

Tom gave me a half smile, shoved his hands in his pockets, then walked away.

I let myself inside the large, dark front entrance. No lights were turned on in the cavernous entryway. I could see a faint glow coming from the living room up ahead. I stood in the hallway and listened.

"No, you've done enough already," said a man's voice.

"Fuck you. You don't know how I feel," Cherry said.

"What did the note say?" asked the voice of an unknown man. I crept closer.

"All it said was how he wanted to end it all, and he didn't want to fake it anymore. I can't believe he fucking did this to me. How could he do this to our daughter?"

"Where is the note, Cherry?" The man's voice sounded pressing, like he had a clenched jaw.

"I gave it to Sgt. McNeil, but I made a photocopy of it. It's upstairs. I'm going to make a recording for his fans," Cherry said as I rounded the corner.

"Can we look at it?" asked a woman's soft voice.

"I don't feel like getting it right now."

The three postmodern rockers looked up at me as I

entered the room. A thin layer of cigarette smoke hung in the air.

"Who are you?" asked the pale, thin, dark-haired man seated next to a curly-haired, tattooed brunette who had her arms around Cherry. The brunette let go of Cherry and quickly picked up and laid a TV Guide over a plate that had a syringe, spoon, and lighter on it.

"Security is supposed to be watching the house. How did you get in?" the brunette asked.

"It's OK. That's my P.I. The good one anyway," Cherry rasped.

I blinked through the smoke-filled room. Was I hearing her right? How high was she? Why wasn't she throwing things and threatening me?

"Cherry, I'm sorry for your loss," I said as I remained standing.

Cherry's make-up smeared, tear-stained face nodded slowly as Kate put her arms back around her shoulders.

"Is there anything you need from me?"

"No, Brittany. I'll have your checks overnighted to you. I just need to be left alone right now."

"I'm headed back to Los Angeles tomorrow morning. If you have any questions for me, please don't hesitate to call me at any of my numbers."

"We won't," said the young man as he glared at me.

11

I heard the melodic rumble of the Impala well before I could see it. Standing in the crowded passenger-pick-up-area of LAX looking for the origin of the noise, I flashed on my dad picking me up from high school at Saint Mary's in his prized possession. I was half surprised when I saw James' wavy-haired framed face behind the wheel, and not the salt and pepper crew cut of a square faced older man.

"It's good to be out of that rain," I said as James kissed me quick on the lips and took my bags to the trunk.

"Alpha will be happy to see you. I have a proposal of what we should do before heading back over the hill."

"Alright, hold that thought. Before we go back to the Valley we need to stop at 1717 Vine Street."

"The high-rise next to the Capitol Records Tower? What for?"

"We're meeting with Genevieve Townsend, Cherry Starlet's attorney."

The I-405 was blessedly free of traffic from the

airport. We arrived with minutes to spare before our appointment.

An attractive blonde in a red skirt suit sat at the center of an administration table centered on the marbled floor, blocking access to the double-sided elevators. Security guards flanked her, one on either side.

"We have an appointment to see Genevieve Townsend."

"Name, please."

"Brittany Wolfe."

"Third elevator on the left side." The woman smiled a mouth full of white-capped teeth as she shook an expensive round pen over her shoulder. "Twenty-eighth floor."

"What's the office number?" James asked.

"Townsend and Lynch *are* the 28th floor." The woman's smile turned noxious as the security guards chuckled.

The sound of the large guards' light laughter was eclipsed by the echo of my heels and James' Salvatore Ferragamo shoes as we crossed the lobby towards the elevators.

"You know who else works with Donatus' and Cherry's managers and label? This woman, Genevieve Townsend," James said.

As we stepped out onto the 28th floor we were surrounded by glass framed-panoramic views of Los Angeles. The floor consisted of wall-to-wall windowed offices. Up close, at best Los Angeles was a butter-faced wide suburban sprawl. Take a step back and it was vibrant, colored, and beautiful. High-rises sparkled, accentuating a sunset that reflected a rainbow thanks to the smog and pollution.

A blonde woman with her hair up in a military style bun click-clacked toward us in short-quick strides dictated by her tight, black pencil skirt. I recognized Genevieve as she got closer.

"Good afternoon, Ms. Wolfe."

"Genevieve, meet my partner James Stacks, another P.I."

"Pleasure. Stacks Private Investigators is your company?"

"No, but it's in the family. I used to practice law, as a civil litigator and defense attorney."

"And now you're a private investigator. Interesting." A few men in suits walked by smiling their hellos. Genevieve gestured for us to follow her. "Let's talk in my office. Please, don't tell any of the staff who you are and why you're here. I also must insist you absolutely do not tell our mutual client of this meeting."

"Of course," we both agreed, however strange.

"Please." Genevieve gestured to a glass door leading to a corner office. Inside was a large oak desk, five leather chairs, and a wall-to-wall fully stocked wet bar complete with sink, silver ice bucket filled with fresh large frozen cubes, mini fridge, and an array of crystal decanters filled at various levels with varying degrees of clear to rose gold liquid.

Genevieve shut the door and sat behind her wood desk and drummed her fingers on the glass top, then paused. She appeared to be studying the glass, her brow furrowed. The entire room smelled of lemon Pledge and Chanel. James and I took a seat across from her.

"Donatus wasn't suicidal."

"What are you saying exactly?" James and I exchanged looks.

"All I'm telling you is when Donatus went missing he was talking to me about getting a divorce and writing Cherry out of his will. He even claimed he could prove infidelity."

"Infidelity? Do you believe that Cherry was having an affair?" I asked.

"I heard rumors; Cherry bed-hopping with other rock stars and bragging about it. It wouldn't surprise me. When Donatus was sent to rehab by a group of his doped-up peers in front of his family it really pissed him off, but he wasn't suicidal."

I clicked on my tape recorder in my purse.

"So, you think it could be murder? Do you think Cherry had anything to do with it?" I asked.

"Right before Donatus' intervention Cherry called me and told me to get her the meanest, most cut-throat divorce attorney I could find. Donatus and Cherry were passionate about each other, but it was a sick love. Cherry knew Donatus for only six months before they were married and she was pregnant by him."

"And her motive?" James asked.

"Motive as old as time. She gets everything. Donatus' entire estate. Donatus never had a chance to cut Cherry out of his will. The media are all over this, and she's name dropping her P.I.s, making it look like she did all she could to find him. Why didn't she go up to Seattle to look for him herself?"

"She told us she had business in LA."

"I know for a fact she didn't have any business in LA, other than that bogus outpatient treatment at the Beverly Hills Peninsula. What a joke. No one was monitoring it and she could leave anytime."

"Why are you telling us all this?" James asked.

"Look," said the attorney. Genevieve handed us each a newspaper.

"Three kids in Paris, two in Australia and a double in Seattle. All copycats. Donatus, the voice of the postmodern generation, reported as a suicide, is already having a chain reaction. Bliss fans are killing themselves." Genevieve stood up, lifted a remote and pointed it at a large corner stereo. "This is why I wanted us to meet at this time."

As the volume rose we could make out Cherry's raspy, tear-soaked voice over the radio.

"This is part of Donatus' note that he wrote for you, his fans. The rest of it was addressed to me, it's personal and it's really none of your fucking business. The part I'll read now was addressed to all of you: *I can't fake it anymore which is why I have to go. How can I play to the roar of the crowd when I no longer have a passion for it?*

"Why couldn't you just enjoy it you son of a bitch? You guys, no one believes suicide is the way to go. When life gets tough you owe it to yourself to live through it."

The rest of the reading of Donatus' suicide note was of similar dialogue - Cherry reading Donatus' words, then interjecting with sorrow and disdain. When Cherry was done, Genevieve powered down the radio.

"I asked Cherry to fax me a copy of that note, and she refused. That letter, it's crucial we see it. I believe all the weirdness, all the nonsensical happenings leading up to Donatus' death have to do with the suicide note. Cherry doesn't know that you're here, does she?"

I shook my head. "No."

"You want us to go back to Seattle and steal a copy of it?" James asked.

Genevieve said nothing, how could she? What attorney could ask that? My guess was that she wanted us to do the majority of the talking. My little tape recorder would pick up very little from Genevieve during this meeting.

"Genevieve, I have to warn you. If what we find puts your client in an unflattering light we're not going to protect her. Keeping Cherry out of jail and protecting her is your job. Our job is to find the truth."

Genevieve continued to say nothing. I waited out her silence. James began to fidget.

"I'll go up to Seattle if she offers me more work, but I won't steal from her. I'll try to find a way to get her to give me a copy of the note. When and if I get it, I'll forward it to you."

Genevieve sighed and shrugged.

"Just do what you can. You'll hear from Cherry

soon. Toyland's new album is going to top the charts with all this publicity. Cherry is about to lead them on a world tour."

I popped in a few speedy pills, chewed them, and James checked his watch as we exited the building.

"Damn. That took longer than I thought. I have to hall ass to my buddy's premiere. He's co-starring in a terrible action movie, and I promised him I'd go. Come with me, Brit. We can suffer the two-hour flick together, then go to the after-party."

I looked down at my dark pantsuit in the sunlight. Was it actually navy blue? I couldn't remember.

"...and I'll take you dress shopping. You're overdue for a present. I can call my buddy Chris to go feed and walk Alpha. We'll shop Rodeo. You'll make all the wanna-be porn stars jealous."

You can take the trust-funded out of the high-rise, but you can't take him out of the lifestyle.

"I can't. The party sounds fun, but I need all my brain cells intact right now. I miss Alpha and my bed. I'll drop you off at your bike in Santa Monica so you won't be late."

I eyed his button-down shirt, khakis, movie star teeth and hair. The slight bend in his nose from one too many fights kept him from looking too perfect. It's not fair. Just add hair product and he's ready to go. For me to be premiere ready involved shopping, make-up, and beauty queen hair. I love the dresses, but hate having to comb my fine, long blonde hair out of a Barbie-doll tease.

"Good to have you back." James embraced and

kissed me once we were out of the car in our office parking lot. As I made my way to the driver's side of my Impala, a hand came down across my ass with a smack. My heart was beginning to race as the cottonmouth set in.

"Damn it, James!"

"You're the only woman who gets that from me, beautiful!"

"Yeah, lucky me. You probably say that to all the bimbos who go out with you, too."

"Brittany Wolfe, I swear, you are the only bimbo in my life," James said, his hand over his heart. He was lucky he was good in bed.

I needed to get home and sit down with my tapes and a notepad if I was going to use this upward high to my advantage.

#

Sitting in traffic on the 405 had me wondering if I should have taken the 5 through downtown instead, one of the many trials and tribulations of living in the Valley. I turned on my radio. Traffic at this speed on uppers is torture; I bet most LA road rage shootings probably had a pharmaceutical explanation.

"Thousands and thousands of Donatus Sun fans showed up to attend the public memorial at the park near Sun's Lake Washington home."

Another snippet of Cherry's tear-stained voice spoke to the crowd. *"I'm so sorry everyone. Now everyone, I want you to say asshole loud. Ready?"* A chorus of assholes vibrated through my car stereo buzzing like a swarm of locusts.

A psychiatrist got on the air. *"Hello, I'm Dr. Hersch. So far there have been more than 20 copycat suicides documented..."*

Holy shit! 20? Already?

"... If you, or if anyone you know is contemplating hurting yourself in any way please call 1-800..." I switched the channel.

"And now for another hour of non-stop Bliss in reverence to the tragic loss of Donatus Sun.

"Oh, Baby doll my mother says I'm lucky to have met you.

She said it was prophesized your aim would be true.

It is now your duty to completely drain me.

You'd do anything they'd want for the right fee,"

Donatus sang from the grave. I listened to the catchy rhythms and riot-like lyrics of Bliss, written by Donatus. Some of the songs were top of the chart singles, some I'd never heard before, all of them were good. The underground exclusivity packaged as mass-market material made it a melodic oxymoron impossible to resist.

12

Thump, thump, thump, thump. I opened my eyes to small bent ears and a black wet nose. My eyes met hers and she whined with anticipation. I looked around at the nest I had made for myself on the couch. I was awake. Alpha leaned down to rest her doggy head next to my pillow so we were face to face. Her tail continued to thump against the floorboards. Maybe if I stayed very still she'd lie down again. Her tongue hung out of her panting grin as she lifted her paw and pressed it to my forehead.

"OK. OK. I'm getting up. You didn't even miss me that much. You just want food." It wasn't the reunion I was expecting with woman's best friend. Alpha was happy to see me, but I could tell she was also looking for signs of James.

I got up off the couch. I had fallen asleep watching MTV replay interviews with Cherry, Donatus and their bands Bliss and Toyland. Tapes, pens, and notepads were scattered everywhere. The character board I had taped to the wall looked like an F.B.I. manhunt investigation presentation.

After jogging with Alpha a good five miles on desert trails, I fixed myself a smoothie, adding a cucumber to top off my berry yogurt and ice. Alpha reluctantly took her green milk bone.

"A moment on the lips, forever on the hips and you're only as young as you look." Oh, my god. Even minus the husband and kids inside my head I still sounded like my mother. Hers is one voice that is hard to get out of your head. I wondered how her fourth marriage was doing. I wanted to see James.

I ran into Starbucks to surprise James with one of his favorite non-fat, vanilla latte things. He would definitely be surprised. I never left the Valley before noon on a weekend.

"That'll be $14.50," said the girl at the register.

Fifteen dollars for a couple coffees and scones?

After parking close by, I walked through the courtyard leading up to James' Westwood condo, almost dropping one of the cups from the cardboard cup holder as my briefcase slid off my shoulder. Two bronzed bikini-clad blondes were already laying out by the pool sunning themselves. I approached the condominium's large oak door, set my briefcase down and knocked. Eyeing the carport on the side of the building I noticed James' bike wasn't there. That was odd. I knocked on the door again and heard some shuffling from the other side.

"I can hear you in there, James. I drove all this way to bring you coffee. Open up. Don't make me get the tear gas."

The front door opened a crack. James stuck his head

and shoulder out. His eyes were red-rimmed from lack of sleep, and if I didn't know any better I could have sworn I smelled alcohol.

"James, who are you talking to sweetie?" asked a woman's nasal voice in a sharp East Coast accent. Bright red acrylic nails gripped the door pulling is past James' hips to reveal Vivian Cask. My heart stuck in my throat. The woman was wearing my bathrobe. Well, technically it was James' bathrobe, but it was the one I wore. Her body filling out the same fabric caused a wave of nausea to run through me. The thought of them touching each other brought hot tears to my eyes that I refused to let fall. James' pants had been thrown on in haste. He had buttoned the top button, zipped up, but left his belt buckle dangling.

"Oh, Brittany. Hi." Vivian laid her head familiarly on James' shoulder, as I stared into his eyes, pained as he winced and recoiled.

"I brought coffee," was all I could say as I set the tray on the porch step, turned, and began to walk away.

"No, Brittany, wait. It's not what it looks like."

I could hear his bare feet break into a run behind me. "Really? 'Cause it looks like Vivian briefed you on more than your uncle's case file. You are a crazy bitch magnet, and you deserve what you get!"

With my briefcase on my shoulder I was running, trying not to let them see me cry. I was almost to the guest parking lot. James had stumbled out the door kicking over the coffee. I looked behind me. Coffee had splashed all over the left leg of James' khakis.

Vivian stood in the doorway, her fake lashes wide open, giving her the surprised face of a cartoon deer. James was intent on grabbing me, half-dressed or not. Good luck asshole. I'd left the Impala unlocked.

"I drank. I fucked up. I barely remember a thing. You know I don't care about her."

I didn't look back this time.

"You fucking asshole!" howled a shrill female New Jersey accent.

"Brittany, wait. Please? I promise, I'll tell you everything that happened."

I didn't want to hear it. Tears were really threatening to fall. I couldn't stand to think what went on between them. He wouldn't have a drink with me, yet he'd party with that vacuous transparently needy trash? Inside my car I revved it before throwing it into reverse. James ran down the manicured rose-bush-lined corridor. I watched him come to a standstill, shirtless, with his hands out pleading. I eyed his disheveled appearance, boxer briefs sticking out of his tan pants; they must have unbuttoned themselves as he was running. A sob caught in my throat. How could I be so stupid, to get with that guy?

It wasn't until I was out on the road a safe distance away that I allowed the tears to flow. Vivian Cask? I didn't even know she was in LA. Had this happened before? Had it been happening the entire time James and I... I couldn't even think about it. She'd been chasing James in that aggressive, East Coast manner reserved for the girls back from his hometown on a mission to become Mrs. James Stacks.

Vivian was office manager for James' Uncle Joe in New Jersey, then met James when he was a drug-addled playboy attorney. She chased him relentlessly. Should I call Joe? A part of me was worried James was using again. The other part of me, the hurt part, the angry part, could really give a shit. If James really was a crazy bitch magnet, what did that make me?

I drove to the gym near the office, and scooped up my gym bag from the trunk. Inside I gave my gym clothes the sniff test. I was instantly relieved I had the foresight to switch out my dirty gym clothes and throw in my new hair dryer.

I hit the weights, lightly. Just because I acted like a man, didn't mean I wanted to look like one. I let my adrenaline sink in while showering. Numb, I was invincible. I dried my long blonde hair shiny straight like a pastel colored *Sweet Valley High* book cover, and after I applied some mascara, took in my youthful appearance. Weight training endorphins had kicked in. I knew I didn't need James to be happy. I didn't need James. I didn't need him to work at Stacks. I was the backbone of the company. Screw him, and not in the pleasurable way. I tried not to remember Vivian touching him. The lump in my throat was coming back.

By the time I found myself back in Hollywood parking in front of the Flamenco Hotel I was back to seeing the world through mournful, dark sunglasses.

I walked past the checkout counter and into the adjacent bar. What about that hideous, red side-paneling and asymmetry of the crumbling bar?

Wouldn't it depress me? I welcomed it.

"Double whisky and Coke, please."

"A bit early, officer," the Lurch lookalike smiled with a mocking head tilt.

"I'm fighting off a cold."

Two whisky and Cokes later and the jagged edges of my run-in with Vivian were nicely sanded down to a less painful, hazy finish.

"Is there a Brittany Wolfe at the bar?" Today the older woman had on a polyester, royal-purple pantsuit and an off-white shirt that looked as if white had been its original color. Her thin hair was rolled up in tiny curlers so tight her head looked like a checkered scalp.

"Thank you. How has your day been?"

The woman squinted at me. "Oh, it's you again. I'm fine, thanks. Do you not have a phone at home?"

"Nope, just a tab at the bar."

The woman sniffed as she followed me into the lobby. I picked up the phone at the front desk.

"Wolfe here."

"Hiya. You weren't in the office, so I thought I'd give the watering hole a try." I listened as Tom exhaled smoke, behind him were subtle sounds of traffic.

"I hope to be glad to hear from you, Tom. You have any news?"

"No new info going around the music circuit, but I was able to get some return phone calls I wasn't really expecting. My buddy is a news gatherer for a few media outlets."

That usually meant dirt supplier who sold ammo to

the highest bidding mud-slinger.

"Cherry and her people have been leaning on the rehab facility Donatus fled from and the hospital in Italy he was admitted to when he OD'd overseas not to talk to the press. Donatus Sun's attorney, Genevieve Townsend herself has sent nasty letters threatening to sue. My buddy was able to find out why."

James could judge him all he wanted. The hard-partying diabetic had the experienced nose of a slow but thorough scent hound. The old dog could sift through piles of manure faster than any of the less seasoned younger ones.

"And?"

"And Cherry making one phone call to the Los Angeles rehab facility before Donatus fled the place like she told the press is a lie. She was logged in by the hospital as having called 15 times. It was noted she was frantic to get a hold of Donatus, and he refused to take her calls. She was written up as threatening to the nurses on staff. At times Cherry pretended to be Donatus' mother, Brianne Knight, or their attorney Genevieve Townsend. Each time she called the nurses kept detailed notes of their interaction with Cherry."

"And the OD overseas?"

"I found the name of the Italian doctor who agreed to speak with me discretely. Contrary to what Cherry told MTV and *Rolling Stone,* Dr. Tribani unequivocally stated it was not a suicide attempt. Dr. Tribani registered the incident as an accidental overdose. Donatus Sun had three Rohypnol, not 50 like Cherry is telling the press. He took them after he celebrated his birthday, drinking a few bottles of champagne with friends. The doctor said with that drug, it could happen to anybody."

"Good to know. Thanks," I said.

"One more thing. I've been seeing reoccurring symbols that are too frequent to be a coincidence. Weird, spook looking guys dressed in black carrying briefcases with a logo of an upright pen balancing scales of justice are everywhere. One I suspect was even tailing me. At first, I thought it was just a new corporate logo, but I've also been seeing this symbol all over performance spots. Spots in Seattle, on some of the Bliss band logos. There's also one of a rainbow with a lightning bolt going through it. It's all reoccurring and weird."

Sounded like the briefcases I saw in the lobby leaving Cherry's room at the Peninsula Hotel. Could it be a new brand of corporate gear?

It was almost sundown as I made my way back to the depressing, dimly lit bar.

"You ready for another?" asked Lurch drying a pint glass with a jaundice-yellow rag.

"Just a cup of coffee please. Thanks."

Lurch smiled obscenely. I felt heat prickle up my back. Just as I was about to reach out and knock the pint glass out of the hunchback's hand I heard a voice.

"Hi there, are you here for the convention?"

The words sounded strange coming from such a young voice. I smelled her before I saw her. It was the sickly sweet smell of cotton candy body spray and baby powder deodorant. Her black fake ponytail was clipped on a bit crooked. Her blue eyes were black with eyeshadow. The barely there green dress was struggling to cling to her painfully thin physique. She couldn't be more than sixteen, eighteen at most.

"Yes, I am. How did you know?" asked a man on the other side of her.

The girl smiled. "Oh, I can tell. You mind some company?"

The man took off his navy blue sport coat. "I'd offer to buy you a drink, but are you even old enough to have one?"

"I don't need one. Do you want an hour or the night?"

The skin under his receding hairline shone in the dim bar light. He began pulling at his necktie and shirt collar. I could tell by the stains growing under the arms of his white button-down that he was burning up.

"I'm not sure what you mean." The man squinted at the young girl, slowly taking in her napkin size dress and towering black heels. His eyebrows began to arch. His eyes widened.

"Look, never mind."

"You're a prostitute, and you think I'd pay to have sex with you?"

The young woman took a step back and shrank. As she turned to leave the man grabbed her arm. I looked back toward the street entrance to see if her pimp was around the corner. The Flamenco wasn't exactly an upscale place.

"Society is suffering due to disease and the

breakdown of house and home. I want a manager!"
The man shouted at Lurch. Lurch picked up a phone
and hit a single call button.

"Let go. Let go!" the girl began to squirm and pawed
at the man with acrylic enhanced nails.

"Over here," Lurch signaled someone I couldn't see.

I pushed my barstool into the man and broke his
grip with my heavy briefcase.

"Well? Run!" I hissed at her.

The young woman blew past me in a shiny green
blur. I'd never seen a woman run so fast in heels. I'd
been a cop. I knew once those girls developed a rap
sheet involving prostitution, that's all they'd ever be,
abused and poor. It made me hate our justice system.
If I was just a little dumber, I would have stayed on
the force.

I flagged down Lurch to get a cup of coffee to go.

"Can I get a coffee to go, black please? I've got to
run."

He eyed me sideways, then turned his suspicious
gaze back to the register. It wasn't until I was back at
my car that I took a sip and noticed it was piss warm.
Asshole. I tossed the cup into a sidewalk trash bin and
headed back to the Valley.

13

The phone rang and I let the answering machine pick it up. When the phone rang again I turned the ringer off. Petting Alpha who laid at my feet, I reached for the blanket on the back of my couch and switched on Music Television. Cherry Starlet was followed by cameras through a park surrounded by hundreds, maybe a thousand, Donatus Sun fans, giving random people hugs. Her smeared, expensive make-up and black lace-edged silk dress that hung off her emaciated body made the unglamorous, flannel-wearing fans look even younger in comparison. Fresh weeds smell better than rotting roses.

I heard my answering machine pick up again and strained to hear what was being said, but couldn't. I'd turned the machine's volume down. Oh hell, I was depressed anyway. I might as well get a drink. I worked already, and it was almost six.

Once I was in the kitchen, I eyed the blinking answering machine. I had 13 voicemails. I pressed play.

"Brittany, just talk to me. You owe me that mu..."

It was James, so I deleted it right away.

"Brittany it's me again...

I didn't bother to listen to the rest and deleted them all. A glint of gold caught my eye on the table; the open invitation to my ex's gala event. The event was tonight and had started two hours ago.

I had already missed dinner and the cocktail hour in Century City, but I still had time to make it to the more intimate, meet-and-greet party hosted in the Hollywood Hills. Would it be a mistake to go? If Ryan and Cynthia Khodorkovsky had broken up I would have heard. I thought of Cynthia and her blonde hair extensions, fake tits, and liposuction waistline. Ugh, those coarse, long, awful doll-like hair extensions. Somewhere a horse was missing a tail. The phone rang again. I was going.

After I fed and took Alpha for a quick jog, I made sure to unlatch the doggy door to the backyard for her guard patrols and pee breaks. After showering I threw on a slinky red dress that had been hanging in my closet with the tags on for weeks; purchased with James in mind. I was wearing the red dress. I blow-dried my hair with a round brush into a long, straight curtain of blonde. After some base, bronzer, mascara, and red lipstick I had the desired effect.

To my relief and shock I only hit traffic once, and that was over the hill leaving the Valley. In a breathtakingly short amount of time I was in Hollywood Hills. As I started the climb up into the Santa Monica Mountains cars lined the neighboring streets and I could hear the joyous laughter, coughs, and chatter of the exclusive party. Surrounded by all the costumes and decoration I felt like I had been transported back in time to Hollywood's silent era. It was then that I started to lose some of my resolve. Was that the press? Would my arrival cause a scene? I was about to turn around and go home when a young valet in an all-white suit and gloves approached my driver's side door and opened it.

"Nice ride! What year is she?"

I fumbled in my purse for the valet ticket. The invitation envelope fluttered to the passenger side floor.

"67," I answered smiling as I handed him the keys.

I adjusted my skintight bright red dress. If the place was packed I could lose myself in the crowd. I walked toward the entrance. Tiki torches lined the brick walls and twinkle lights glittered in the bushes. Hieroglyphs were etched into the sand colored brick of the hillside mansion. Such amazing execution. The yard and entryway smelled of sweet jasmine and fresh cut roses from the various, colorful vine-entwined bouquets.

"May I see your invitation, please?" asked a tall tan man dressed in black.

I searched my clutch. Oh, no. It must have been in the envelope that was now on the floor of my car. I looked around for a valet.

"I'm sorry, mam. This party is invitation only. Can I have your name please?" The man put a hand to the headphone in his ear. "Get ready to list check, over."

"Yes, I know. I left my invitation in my car. I'm

friends with Ryan Kemp. My name is Brittany Wolfe."

"Did you get that, Jimmy?" said the man into his palm.

Couples sipping champagne were stopping to observe the doorman and me, probably bored and looking for some action. Out of the corner of my eye an older woman in a gold sequins dress smirked.

Another white-gloved man with the same Roman soldier haircut came and stood by the other one's side. "I'm sorry. This is a private event." I looked up at him. His orange-tanned blue eyes under black-rimmed Armani glasses were all business. This one was the muscle. "I'm going to have to ask you to leave."

I began to turn around and walk away.

"Brittany, you made it!" said a male voice.

Breaking away from a gaggle of women who showed plenty of bronzed skin wrapped in sparkly skintight dresses was a tall, wavy-gold-haired man with a well-groomed five o'clock shadow. The man strode up to me as he held aloft a flute of champagne as if it were an award.

"Ryan? I'm sorry. I can't find my invitation."

"She's with me."

"Nice to meet you. Please enjoy." The man in black held out his hand and gestured me a belated welcome.

"Thank you," I said. Manners cost nothing. What dicks.

Ryan's groupies followed him toward me, but after he held out his arm so I could place my hand on his bicep they hung back.

"I'm so glad you're here. Have you ever been to this

place before?" asked Ryan.

I shook my head trying to tell if he was kidding.

"Let me show you something spectacular!"

I followed Ryan's lead. A man walked by with a wine bottle and a napkin. "Excuse me, sir?"

Ryan handed me his champagne and scooped up a free glass off a nearby table. "Half glass of red stuff please."

The man poured Ryan his red, wiping the edge of the bottle carefully with his white napkin. I followed Ryan to a closed patio. He took out a key and unlocked the glass door.

"Isn't it something?"

I took a sip of my champagne and looked out at the joyously bright smog enhanced sunset.

"We used to watch a lot of sunsets together." Ryan took a long pull from his ruby filled glass.

I nodded, staring out at the purple, red, orange and gold colors. The terrible air quality from a multitude of pollutants gave LA amazing sunsets. Ryan had been poor, and I was frustrated with work as a police officer. Drinking together we would laugh, fight, have sex, fight, and watch sunsets. Back then we wanted to forget about our jobs and everything else. We were different people.

"Where's Cynthia? Don't you guys like live together now?"

Ryan frowned and took a gulp from the wine glass he was holding.

"I had a driver take her home." He checked his watch. "With any luck she's passed out by now."

"Did she drink too much at the party?"

Ryan nodded. "For the last couple of days."

"Things aren't working out with you two?"

Ryan was quiet. I put my hands on the brick wall and imagined Joan Crawford, Greta Garbo, and Betty Davis standing in the same spot, staring at the sunset. The sunset wouldn't have been half as beautiful. The air was cleaner then.

I felt Ryan's arm wrap around my waist and as I tilted my head back, I felt my face warmed by the setting sun. I waited for what I knew was coming. Ryan was a great kisser. That's when I felt wet liquid began to pour down my dress.

"Damn it, I'm sorry," said Ryan. Half of his glass of wine was down my dress. "Quick, follow me."

I took his hand and let him lead me off the patio and into a narrow hallway. A camera, a few lights, and a man wearing headphones while holding a boom-stick stood next to another man holding a mic.

"Ryan! Ryan Kemp, the man of the hour. Are you available to do a brief interview? Is it true you'll be making a cameo appearance in the upcoming film?"

A flash went off from somewhere down the hall, and all I could see were bright lights for half a minute.

"Who's this?"

"This is my friend Brittany Wolfe, she helps with my mystery novels. She used to be a member of LAPD and..."

"She's the private investigator for Cherry Starlet! Brittany, can we ask you a few questions?"

"Ryan, I can't talk to the press." I squeezed his hand.

"Just a moment. We'll be back," Ryan smiled, flashing his freshly bleached even teeth. He pulled me down a hall opposite the cameras. Halfway down he pulled out another key. He unlocked the door and we stepped into a bedroom that looked like a time portal. The linens were fresh; the old, heavy wood furniture well oiled, but it was a room designed to look from the Orient in all its 1920s redwood and mother-of-pearl detailed glory.

"Cherry Starlet? You're working for Donatus Sun's widow?"

"Yeah. It's pretty crazy."

Ryan disappeared into the private bathroom and emerged with a towel. "I hope you can make the time to catch me up. I've missed you. Damn, Brittany. I've been so bored. Remember when we would spend whole weekends in bed?"

I patted my cleavage and dress. Good thing I was wearing red. The wine stain looked so intentional people probably assumed I was wearing couture. I more than remembered our marathon weekends. We'd drink wine wrapped in each other's arms. Come Monday we'd be fighting again, mostly due to Ryan's mood swings. I took a step away from him.

"Sorry, Brittany." Ryan moved toward the door to leave. "And sorry about the wine."

"Don't go."

My arms encircled his neck as he leaned down to kiss me. I leaned into the kiss, my tongue pushing against his until his breath caught in his throat. He quickly drew his breath back in taking mine out of my lungs. I gasped. My heart beat faster as he pressed into me.

"How does Cynthia touch you?" I asked.

"Don't. Don't talk about her," Ryan said.

"About your girlfriend? Excuse me, your fiancée who's about to be your wife?"

"You were my girlfriend. You were supposed to be my wife."

His lips crushed against mine, Ryan began pulling off his left black leather shoe with the toe of the other. Hurried and without looking, he lifted his right foot to unlace the other shoe with his left hand as he kept his right arm wrapped around my waist. I heard the second shoe drop and then the rustling noise of his belt buckle. His tie hung loosely around his neck as he began to step out of his pants as he finished opening his shirt. His chest looked more sculpted than I remembered. His growing fame must have pushed him to work out harder than before. Vanity, my favorite sin in a man.

Still kissing, I sat on the bed, letting my heels slip off and fall to the floor. Before lying on my back, Ryan slipped my dress straps over my shoulders, pulling it down to my ankles.

Frenzied now, Ryan immediately attacked the back of my strapless bra. I sat up a bit, conscious of the presentation. With two hands, I unhooked the front clasp of my bra. Ryan's mouth sought out any remaining wine. The smell of his hair, the familiar weight of him, all the memories of our time together raced through my head.

His tongue trailed down my stomach as he lifted up my knees, causing me to lean back. Through the background music and women's laughter, I could hear people walking back and forth in front of the room and exiting in and out the front door.

Kissing my knees as he removed all obstructions, I felt his stubble tickle the inside of my thigh and I gasped. It was like his mouth was on all of me as he worked enthusiastically. I tried to keep my own enthusiasm quiet as I gripped the sheets of the bed.

I began to buck in tiny motions. I could no longer contain the noise.

His eyes closed as his right hand guided him into me. My insides were shuddering. I gripped onto him as the headboard banged against the wall, picking up in noise and speed. My entire body shuddered. Smiling, Ryan ran his fingers through my hair as I shuddered through a few more pleasurable after-shocks.

Resuming his rhythm, Ryan reassured himself aloud, "It's alright. It's alright.". Ryan's face screwed up tight as he groaned, as if he were trying to bench press his own weight.

He collapsed on top of me as we tried to catch our breath.

Trying to breath with his body collapsed on top of me was impossible. I pushed him off and rolled onto his chest. Panting, I brushed my no longer perfect blonde hair onto my back to avoid soaking up the sweat from his chest.

"Everybody heard that," I said.

"Hell yeah they did." Ryan laughed.

"I need to find a way to sneak out of here."

"No worries, my lady. I won't mar your precious reputation."

"Oh, shut up. What about Cynthia?"

I leaned over to pick up my bra as Ryan reached to grab for his shirt, causing us to bump heads. Ryan laughed out loud.

"Shhh, I'm not kidding. What if Cynthia found out?" I cautioned him, eyeing the door leading back out to the party.

"What about her?"

"You're engaged!"

"That's about to be broken off."

Oh. Shit.

"Ha... not on my account." I eyed the door.

"No, many other reasons, but I'm happy you came," Ryan said.

"Me, too." I meant it.

Ryan took both my hands in his and sighed. We were both perfectly miserable. Two hearts are better than one, to lean on.

14

The drive back into the Valley took a lot longer than the drive out of it. I didn't mind. I was high recalling my encounter with Ryan. Impulsive reunions always felt the most exciting and the most satisfying.

Once I got to my house my heart flipped. Alpha was outside wagging her tail behind the gate, and right in front of her were my favorite flowers, like the bouquets that were at Ryan's party. I picked up the bushel of lilies, roses, and baby's breath and looked at the card. My heart hardened.

Let's talk. - James

I took them inside as Alpha bounded after me. Inside, Alpha flopped down in front of me; I gave her some vigorous belly rubs, then put the flowers in water. Just because they were from James didn't mean they couldn't remind me of Ryan.

That night was the first time I'd slept soundly in my bed for a full eight hours in some time. Alpha snored gratefully next to the bed in her brown, cushioned dog bed on the floor, although I heard her growl occasionally as I drifted off to sleep.

I woke up and smiled at the sun shining through my window. I had almost forgotten how a full night's sleep could change one's perspective. I felt hopeful that sex with Ryan, finished laundry, and an extra cup of coffee with a drop of bourbon were the cure for getting over James, and they were, until I found a pair of his cargo pants jammed between my washer and dryer.

The moment I rolled my suitcase out from underneath my bed Alpha began to whine and follow me around the house. Once I was done packing I laid down on the couch and took a nap with her until Anne Marie got there.

"I shouldn't be more than a few days, and the sheets on the bed are clean."

"Great. No worries. Hiya Alpha," Anne Marie scratched my drooling dog behind the ear. That simple gesture usually made me feel less bad as Alpha whined throughout my walk out the door and to my car. I made a mental note; I would make it up to her with a camping trip to Ventura Beach when I got back.

After sliding my suitcase into the back seat, I sat down in the Impala's driver's seat and turned the key in the ignition. Hard rock blasted from the front speakers. I yelped and turned the volume dial to its off position. I took a few deep breaths to calm my heart rate. Someone was in my car. Who could have, or would have done that? Was it a message? I kept my car unlocked when the gate was closed. Anyone could have climbed the fence. Like, Trisha. She was just crazy enough to harass me. Maybe there was a way to sic her on Vivian. Was I the only non-obsessed woman James had been with?

I'd already caught Trisha staking out my place the day she attacked James. Her long brown hair and innocent blue eyes, she would hardly have drawn suspicion creeping around my yard. James was an idiot to play with the emotions of a woman so young and intense. I didn't bother to shut the car door as I jumped out and ran to the front gate to look around for Trisha's car. There was no sign of her. She wasn't across the street, or near the park. Still, I felt someone watching me. I looked back at the house; Anne Marie and Alpha stood in the front window. Alpha continued to whine as I waved goodbye.

A cup of coffee and two glasses of cheap Chardonnay later, I was landing back at Sea-Tac. I took a Valium and an energy pill in line at the car rental office. My LA smog-coated sun had been replaced by the crisp, clean deluge of Seattle rain.

"It's impossible to get a flight to Portland and Seattle now. Every time my admin tries to make reservations all of first class and business are booked up by the music label execs and managers looking for the next Bliss." The young, white man in a grey suit said to the older white man in a navy suit as I stood behind them in line.

Driving to the outskirts of Seattle I went straight to Cherry's lake front manor before going to a hotel. I told Cherry I would be in either tonight or early tomorrow. With all her dramatic storytelling, I needed to catch her off guard before she had the chance to insulate herself in another cocoon of famous, paranoid, drug-addled artist friends.

When I arrived in front of the three-story home I was surprised to see only one media van parked on the street. It was eye-of-the storm quiet. The rain had stopped briefly, and I could hear the crackle of leaves blowing over the walkway as I rolled down the window of my rental.

"Hello?" Asked a woman's voice through the call box.

"Hi, Cherry. It's Brittany."

The black iron gate buzzed, I heard it unlatch, and it slowly swung open. "Let yourself in. I'm on the second floor."

I parked near the entrance, next to the fountain that wasn't running today. As I walked through the first floor a thin haze of cigarette smoke hung in the air and grew thicker as I walked up the stairs.

"Cherry?" I looked down at the door leading to Little Chris' room.

"I'm in the master bedroom," Cherry called down to me. I followed the voice up to the dual white French doors. Cherry lay reclining on her pink satin, pillow-covered California king, the same bed under which Synroc and I had found the bag of Rohypnol. Wrapped in a black lace robe over a barely-there tank top, silk shorts, and knee-high stockings, she leaned back. Her closet doors were open; clothes hung with expensive price tags attached, and unopened shiny shoe boxes were stacked chest high in corners. Cherry didn't look up from the composition notebook she was scribbling in.

"Hi, Cherry. How are you doing?"

"Fine."

"Who's that?" I asked pointing at a picture of a young woman holding a small child in a frame on the nightstand near Cherry's bed.

"That's my daughter."

"Who's the woman with her?"

"She was our nanny before Little Chris. I don't remember her name."

The young woman looked like she could have been the mother of the fresh-faced toddler. Blue eyes smiled beneath the bangs of her long, blondish-brown hair. Her clothes looked cheap and old, but there was an exuberance about her. There was a fresh innocence in the way she held the small child that displayed the happiness between them. As Cherry coughed a bit, her chest rose and fell under her expensive black lace. Fresh weeds smell better than decaying roses.

"How are you? I heard your reading of Donatus' letter on the radio.
"

"You did?" Cherry rubbed her stocking feet together almost like a child. "I've been OK. I just want to stay working. I need to work." Cherry stared up at the ceiling. "Tonight, I'm going to a Camille Paglia reading."

I raised an eyebrow.

"She's a feminist cultural critic. I love her. How

come your partner never comes up to Seattle with you?" Cherry asked.

"He had business to attend to."

"He's too pretty, that one. I expect P.I.s to be hard-assed and carved out of wood."

James being a pretty boy was a common misconception.

"In his letter, Donatus said he was lying with his guitar on the bed, but the bed wasn't touched when Synroc and I searched it."

"No, Brittany." Cherry sighed and pulled at one of her stockings. "I said, I was lying on the bed."

"But it sounded like Donatus was saying he was lying on the bed, which would mean someone else would have had to remake the bed. I'll ask Sgt. McNeil to let me see the note." I'd played my trump card. Cherry didn't know the police weren't even entertaining the idea of cooperating with me.

"No, Brittany. That would be a waste of time." Cherry reached under one of her over-priced satin pillows and handed me a piece of crumpled computer paper. "You can look at this copy. The police have the original."

It was a good-sized note. The page was filled with scribble. I held it aloft in my hand, then steadied my eyes on Cherry.

"I need to get my reading glasses. Just a moment."

I exited the room and walked down the stairs quickly. Once in the office I switched on the large printer. I cringed as it loudly warmed itself up.

"Brittany?" I could hear a hint of panic

upstairs.

I made a photocopy and slipped it into my briefcase. Still holding my briefcase, I went back upstairs. Cherry was sitting straight up in bed, her arms hugging a small, black ruffled pillow in a pensive grip. I handed her back the copied note.

"Well?"

"I don't have my glasses on me. I'll have to look at it later."

"I'd make you a copy, but the office copier isn't working too well. It needs more ink or something. Maybe tomorrow I can have it fixed."

"That won't be necessary. It worked fine for me just now. I have a copy in my briefcase."

I stared into her eyes, and she stared back unwavering.

"Good. That's good." Cherry leaned back.

The brand new blue plastic Mustang I rented wasn't too bad, but I preferred the Honda. The newer muscle cars weren't very muscular. I threw my briefcase into the trunk next to my suitcase, then locked the trunk and went back inside. I didn't trust setting my briefcase down in the house. Cherry had many entities on her payroll, and my copy of the note and my tape recorder were items of interest.

Cherry was walking down the stairs as I re-entered the house and motioned for me to follow her into the living room. Would she have another one of her famous temper tantrums? Cherry sat down on a chocolate suede couch. She crossed her legs. Very pale in her black outfit, she appeared thinner than she had a week ago. Only remnants of washed-off make-up clung to the ends of her lashes, the outline of her lips and the hallows of her cheeks. She pulled out a folded piece of blue paper and held it out toward me. I stood up and took it.

"That should cover you through to the end of the month. On the back of the check is the gate code to let yourself in when you need to. I want to know where Donatus was, who he was with, what he was doing the last four days before he died, and I want to know everything."

I took the check. It was more than generous, but why? This was a woman who had sent death threats to journalists just for writing unflattering reviews. She hired us to find her husband before he could hurt himself, and now he was dead. Why wasn't she livid pissed? I wasn't ready to jump to conclusions; grief does funny things to people, but why wasn't she angry?

Cherry lifted her feet up under her on the couch, then smoothed out her robe over her pale thighs.

"I've been getting calls from *Rolling Stone* and *Vanity Fair*. They want to interview you," Cherry said, her eyes intent on mine.

Genevieve warned me of this.

"I'd prefer to limit my interaction as much as possible during our on-going investigation."

"That makes sense. Yes, of course. I'd like you to come with me to our cabins up north before you head back to LA. How does tomorrow sound?"

I borrowed a phone book from a bar near the lake

front, and booked a hotel downtown. It was a little fancier than the last one but hell, it was a business expense, and with what was in my pocket, Stack's Private Investigators could afford it.

I arrived at my room, briefcase in hand. Valet had taken my rental, and the bellman would be up with my suitcase. I took in my downtown view. The bathroom was nice. A Jacuzzi tub had my name on it, but first I'd hit the gym downstairs. After tipping the bellman a couple bucks for bringing up my bag, I sat on my turned-down king size bed and made a phone call.

"Hi Tom. I'm at the Sheraton. Can you meet me at the bar in three hours?"

"I can do four."

"Sounds good," I said lying on the king size bed and playing with the remote.

Tom coughed. "Sheraton, huh? It pays to be on Cherry Starlet's payroll.

I winced. "See you soon."

"Bye."

Once I finished my workout I sneaked into an open conference room. As usual, they had continental breakfast leftovers in the kitchenette area. I carried my packet of oatmeal and a yogurt back up to the privacy of my room. I enjoyed the downtown view as I ate my stolen meal. No matter what kind of check was in my pocket, I couldn't bear to pay for something I knew could be foraged for free.

I heated water in the coffee maker and had a seat on the couch next to the bed. The large TV had more stations than I was used to. I flipped through. Every channel was the R.I.P. Donatus Sun station. I clicked up to the 5:00 news.

"The Phenomenon continues. Donatus Sun was a voice for the downtrodden; throw teenage angst alongside Donatus Sun's suicide and it spells out a worldwide disaster. From Australia to Japan young people are committing suicide. Donatus' rocker wife, Cherry Starlet has a message for all of them."

The shot went from the pretty news anchor to the bleach blonde bob of Cherry Starlet's red-lipped face framed by black-tinted Chanel sunglasses.

"Don't listen to the, *it's better to burn out than fade away* nonsense. Life is hard on us all, but we owe it to ourselves to live it. Suicide is a long-term solution to a short-term problem."

There you had it. Attorney Genevieve Townsend's voice coming out of her client's mouth. Clips of Cherry were all over television.

I flipped back to MTV.

"This just in. Toyland's bass player, Kristie White, was found dead in her apartment today of an apparent overdose. Frontwoman Cherry Starlet-Sun gave a statement from her Seattle estate." They're throwing in the Sun after Starlet now.

Standing on her front porch wrapped in a big green coat I could see she still had on the same black tank top that she wore when I had left her house earlier.

"We have lost two very talented, wonderful souls so close to each other," Cherry sobbed. "All we can do is keep working. That's what they would have wanted us to do. Keep moving forward."

"Do you have anything to say about mistakes? Cherry, how do you survive the past?" asked a reporter off-camera as camera flashes sparked from every angle.

"I've done so many stupid things in the past. I mean, I was with Red Erickson for Christ's sake. He would have been nothing without me."

The shot went back to the MTV news anchor. *"Already outside for the start of Robotic Tension's Seattle show tonight we caught up with lead singer Red Erickson to see what he had to say about Cherry's message."*

The red-headed man wore a black t-shirt and had a guitar strapped to his back. He laughed as he listened to Cherry insult him. "She's still a heartless bitch – bleep-." The monitored censor was one word off every expletive; the second-too-late censoring only covered muted pauses.

"But, wouldn't you say Cherry's changed since she's become a mother? She's no longer the same woman who ended up in jail," said the reporter.

Red Erickson took the mic and faced the camera. "Yes, but a softer, kinder Charlie Manson is still fucking –bleep- Charlie Manson. Cherry, I don't care if you are Jesus and your lawyers are the twelve disciples. Don't fuck –bleep- with me. I never crossed you, and you've crossed me now."

The camera connected back to the one in front of Cherry's home, where fans had gathered.

"What do you think of Red Erickson's response?"

"Clearly, he's a wanker," replied a red-mouthed blonde in a Cagney accent.

"Yeah, she just lost her husband and her bass player, man," said a plump young man wearing a Bliss t-shirt.

I looked down at my watch. A bath was out of the question. I showered quickly, threw on some make-up and blow-dried my hair. I chose a black shirt, red tank-top, heels, and a blazer. With any luck, there'd be a cute guy to flirt with at the bar after my meeting with Tom.

There was a knock at my door. That was strange. I wiped the excess hair product from my hands and opened the door.

"Hi, Tom?"

"Hi, Brittany…" Tom sighed. His eyes squinted in discomfort as he pulled at his shirt collar, his already strained buttons threatened to pop. He eyed me sideways. Was that him looking guilty?

"Tom, what is it?"

"Hi, Brittany." James poked his head in, his blue eyes wide, hands shoved in his pockets with tension. A newspaper was rolled under his arm.

15

"Why is he here?" I asked Tom refusing to look at James. It hurt too much.

But James was already in front of the door.

"I have nothing to say to you." I began to shut it, but it only collided with James' shoulder and raised knee.

"No, Brittany. You'll hear me out. Nothing happened."

"OK. Right. Why was she wearing *my* bathrobe?"

"*Your* bathrobe?" James asked.

"Screw you."

"I love you, Brittany," James said, continuing to shove the door. It didn't take long for the door to take his side.

"I hate you." I could call security, but he was my boss' nephew. If he was arrested in Seattle I would have some embarrassing explaining to do. Frankly, I'd suffered enough for this indiscretion. He was inside and there was nothing I could do. "James, please leave."

"I didn't have sex with Vivian. She's a snake, and she scares the shit out of me. I already have one woman stalking me. I learned my lesson with Trisha. The moment Vivian told me she was collecting baby clothes I knew not to touch her."

Weird. - "Next you'll tell me you didn't drink either."

"That's what you have to let me explain. I wish you had gone to that party with me. Vivian was there, and she kept handing me these fruity drink things. The next thing I know I'm hammered. She took me home and I was probably dead from the waist down. When I woke up I was in my clothes on the floor next to my couch."

"Now, it's my fault for not attending? I can't babysit you, damn it. And that's no excuse. I drink, and I would have never done that to you."

"Oh, yeah?" James held out the paper he had been holding. There was a picture of Ryan and me, his arms around my shoulders standing on the balcony of the mansion in the Hollywood Hills. The headline read: *What's The Mystery of Their Relationship? - New York Times bestselling mystery novelist, Ryan Kemp, and detective to the stars, Brittany Wolfe, together at his gala book signing."*

"James, please just go," a giant lump grew in my stomach as I felt my face flush. I needed my heart to calm down. I wondered how sneakily I could cop a benzo out of my purse.

"Look, look. Are you seeing that unpredictable writer again? Is this a real thing, Brittany?" His blue eyes looked so sad and beautiful in that desperate way all handsome men have when their strong faces fall.

Was this how Cherry made Donatus?

"You're considered a celebrity detective now. People from all over LA have been calling our office asking to hire you. Even though you're unavailable, business has picked up," James said.

Cherry's voice ruminated in my head. – "We're going to be like Sid and Nancy." – And they were, only I had studied that case. Sid didn't kill Nancy, but Cherry probably thought he did. Sid, aka Simon Ritchie, was out cold on Dilaudid when a blond haired, blue-eyed drug-addled psycho named Michael stabbed her, and took $38,000 and $500 worth of drugs off her person. The NYPD gave just as much of a shit about the Chelsea as Seattle cops did about alternative rock gods. Sid was brutally raped in jail before being released on bond and dying of an overdose. I could piece together how Cherry's mind worked. Sid's own mother gave him the fatal dose and admitted it on her death bed. If you want to get away with murder, you kill a junkie.

James kissed me, and I let him. It was taking me some time to respond. My stomach churned with guilt. James couldn't wait, already panting.

"All I've done is think about you. I dream about you. I don't know what I'd do if I lost you."

It was the addict talking again. By the time my skirt was up over my waist I was ready. We kissed like that, with my back against his chest; he lifted me up against him faster. After, I barely had time to brush my teeth before James was carrying me back to bed.

I opened my eyes. The phone rang to give me my

wake-up call. I got up and slipped into one of the hotel's terry cloth robes. Once my headphones were in place I went through my tapes. Both Cherry's and Genevieve Townsend's voices rang clear as a bell. When the coffee maker was done I already had the copy of Donatus' suicide note on the desk in front of me along with the articles with my name in them.

I thought about what James had said, "You're considered a celebrity detective now. People from all over LA have been calling our office asking to hire you. Even though you're unavailable, business has picked up."

I read through the note, slowly this time. It looked legit.

Bowing Out –

I haven't been able to nurture my relationship to art and music for some time now. Lately I've just been going through the motions. The nameless faceless roar of the crowd does nothing for me. It's been this way the last two tours, and it's unbearable. Nothing moves me, which has terrified me to the point of being barely able to function. This is why I have to say goodbye. Don't worry. It's not forever. I hope and pray it's not. I've had it so good, and don't think that my turning away from this success is about me being ungrateful, because that's not true. I am eternally grateful, but like a character from a Patrick Suskind novel I am distrustful of humans to the point of pure hatred. When I see the dog eat dog lack of empathy this industry inspires it's hard to believe we're even the same species.

It's better to burn out than to fade away, so now it's time to say goodbye.

Forever in your orbit,
Donatus Sun
Cherry, please be stronger than me, for our daughter
who'll be so much better without me. My love to you both.

What stuck out to my trained eye right away was
the address, *Bowing Out*, and the last lines after his
signature - written in large scrawl, while the rest of the
note was written in cramped, tiny lettering. It could
have been the result of a drug-induced state while
finishing the letter.

"What are you doing?"

"About to order up breakfast. Were you serious
about people calling to hire me since my name's been
in the papers?"

"Oh, yeah. They call for you, but still hire from the
company. You've made Stack Private Investigators the
detective service for the stars. Uncle Joe's in heaven."

"Get up so we can get a jump on the day. It'll take
Cherry some time to get ready to show us the cabins."

"Come over here first."

I could skip my workout this morning.

After breakfast James and I dropped off my car, and
I hopped into his rental, a Lincoln Town Car.

Once at the lake front manor, I handed James a
scrap of paper with the key code from my pocket so he
could key.

"Is it what you were expecting?" I asked.

"The place looks exactly like it did on TV."

I eyed the view. A couple television news vans were
staking out the Sun residence.

James and I approached the door, and were surprised when Cherry swung it open. She was wearing low-rise ripped jeans and a black halter top. Her platinum hair was clipped back in wooden barrettes and she had on hiking boots and wore a small military style backpack. Her eyeliner was flawless. So, this is how rock stars dress to go visit their cabins in the woods.

"Cherry, you remember my partner, James?"

Cherry squinted at him. "Oh yeah. The handsome one." A woman with dark, blood-red hair cropped into a pixie cut stepped out from behind Cherry. "This is my drummer, Jenny Lawless. She's coming with us."

"I made these," Synroc came to the door and handed Cherry and Jenny two to-go cups. I really hoped we weren't driving around two open containers with these two.

"Thanks, Syn. God knows why we ever fucking broke up," Jenny said taking hers.

"I caught you fucking my drummer in our recording studio during my birthday party," Synroc said. He looked back into the manor and sneered.

"Oh yeah," Jenny said. "That was a great party."

James got into the driver's side and the two women slid into the back. I took a seat in the passenger side, and Cherry leaned into Jenny. It was like James and I weren't even there.

"I still can't believe you had sex with that drummer, Steve," Cherry said to Jenny. "Why?"

"Because he's a tiny little man, and I was still hoping he was magical. No, really, he came up to me in the dark and I thought he was my boyfriend. He was massaging me and rubbing my back. It felt so good. I should have known it wasn't Syn," Jenny sighed.

"You called and confirmed we got the suites comped in London? You're sure they agreed to separate rooms?"

"Yes, Cherry. I told you. Manager Steve took care of everything."

"Fuck, Jen I just want you to follow up. Uh, James? You know to go east from here, right?"

"I can get us to Carnation, but then you have to direct me to the cabins once we're close."

"I'm going to build one of those in-home Buddhist shrines like Tina Turner and Uma Thurman have. It would be a nice place to put Donatus' ashes."

"You're having him cremated?" James asked.

"Yes, it's what he wanted."

Even after the forest grew dense and houses became sparse Cherry continued talking non-stop about her plans and tally taking.

"We can't focus on global popularity now. It's the kiss of death for bands who get big this fast. We have to gig locally; Toyland's biggest support is here, at home," Cherry continued with her career obsessed banter.

"I'm totally aware I have lots of enemies. I kind of enjoy the attention, in a way. It's like I can feed off it."

"Did you ever hear back about who reported to the press that you overdosed?" Jenny asked.

Cherry frowned. "That son of a bitch who gave the story to the Associated Press won't know what hit him when I'm through. I'm going to find that asshole and sue him. I can prove I was at the Peninsula Hotel. People saw me there. It's a total lie."

James and I looked at each other.

"You told us you planted the story." James reminded Cherry.

Jenny nearly choked. "You're still pulling that crap? Cherry, really? And with all that's been happening?"

"What? No. They're confused with something else."

Cherry glared at us through the rearview. Her eyes said it all. It was clear we had been hired to drive to the investigation site and to keep quiet.

"Left, no right. No, shit, sorry, left."

"Hadn't you been doing construction here a lately?" James asked.

"Yes, but I usually don't drive. Here we are, his and hers. Donatus built the new cabin for me as a wedding present."

"Only because you complained constantly about his cabin," Jenny said.

"Because it was completely gross, and he wouldn't let a maid go in and touch the place. His man cave was a place for him to write music, paint and sculpt. Every time someone touched his stuff he was convinced we'd had another break in."

The weather was oppressively damp and cold. The new cabin dwarfed the old one. The weathered old house looked like a cabin, the newer one was painted white and looked like an unfurnished glass palace. Their cabins mirrored their clashing personalities.

Cherry's reminded me of a life-sized version of the

Barbie mansion that a wealthy cousin of mine had. I wanted one more than anything, but made do with the Barbie camper my father found for me at a swap meet. It was missing pieces, and we never could get the $1 written in black Sharpie pen off its side. Still, I loved it.

Now, I was standing in front of a life-sized version of my cousin's Barbie palace. Through the front of the house, I could see a pool beyond the white-columned windows. The sunlight off the water produced rippling sapphire shadows on the white walled interior. In contrast, the weathered old cabin had an old brick smoke stack on top of a heavy, oak exterior complete with chipped, green-painted shutters that blended with the forest.

A newly constructed bridge connected the old cabin with the new over a fast-moving creek. The new white palace soaked up most of the sun's rays, leaving much of the old cabin in shade. The white mansion was still under construction. It looked vacant but was still a clear exhibition of success and wealth. Donatus' cabin looked like something the staff to Cherry's palace would live in.

We entered Donatus' cabin, which was one story with a loft on a second floor. In the chill of the shade the cabin's damp interior smelled of mildew.

"Donatus usually slept up here," Cherry said. She and Jenny began climbing up the stairs as James and I stayed downstairs to look around the living room and kitchen area.

There were drop clothes - a rainbow of paint-splattered sheets, easels, paints, and unfinished canvasses scattered about.

CD cases littered the space around the stereo system. Oddly proportioned baked dolls, some shaped liked fetuses, laid in a pile on one of the windowsills. A guitar stand holding up five different guitars stood in a corner next to a large amplifier and a mess of chords. I noticed a jacket and other clothing spread around the living room and tossed across the backs of kitchen chairs.

I poked through a large box. After switching on an overhead light, I could see what was giving off such a strong organic, musky odor. There was a thin layer of moss covering everything, even the guitars. The large box was filled with music magazines. I eyeballed about 50.

I looked over at James. Without saying a word, I knew he was thinking the same thing. Donatus might have been an unapologetic slob, but a rock star junkie wouldn't sleep in these conditions. Both of our noses were scrunched up as we took it all in. I followed James upstairs. The moss wasn't as thick upstairs, probably because the upstairs was open to multiple streams of sunlight and ventilated split beams. The loft was bare except for a large futon.

Cherry walked up to me and reached into her coat pocket. She pulled out a cloth pouch.

"Look, Brittany. Donatus was here," she said removing a syringe.

"Cherry, there's moss on everything downstairs. You can tell nothing's been touched for a while. He didn't come here from rehab."

Cherry's brows knitted together as Jenny began checking under the futon's pillows.

"Well, I can't find anything. Where's the bathroom?" Jenny asked.

"Downstairs to the left of the kitchen." Cherry turned back to face me as Jenny began her dissent. "Look, I know he was here. He must have hung out here for a few days, then gone back to our lake front property. I've taken some cigarette butts to have them analyzed for prints. I'll prove he was here." She held the syringe under my nose. "I know how his mind works when he's using. He always…"

A shrill scream erupted from below. We all rushed downstairs. With James in front, Cherry and I ran into the bathroom to find Jenny and James staring into the toilet. Jenny covered her mouth with both her hands.

James held the back of his hand to his nose.

"You girls don't want to see this."

"Let me through!" Cherry pushed past him in a huff, then shrieked. I peered over her shoulder into the toilet. Three putrefied, bloated dead rats bobbed in a circle inside. They had clearly been in there for quite some time. If Cherry didn't plant that new syringe upstairs, someone else did.

"Ugh!" Cherry threw the cloth containing the syringe and cigarette butts into the bathroom waste basket.

16

Genevieve was waiting for us by the elevator door when the doors opened.

"How did it go with Cherry?" she asked.

"She didn't try to bludgeon me with anything."

Genevieve looked through the glass door of a man's office, smiled, and waved. The man in a dark blue suit waved back at us as he peered around his computer.

"Let's talk in my office."

We followed her into her corner room and she gestured politely to the wet bar. I helped myself to a scotch and soda as James opened a Diet Coke from mini fridge. Genevieve took a seat in her large leather chair and shuffled papers.

"Where you able to look at the note?"

I pulled my copy for her in its manila envelope. After removing the copied letter from its sheath, I handed it over and her mouth dropped open in a silent o.

"Does she know you have this?" Genevieve asked.

"Yes, I told her. It's a copy of a copy. The cops have the original. I didn't tell her until after I visited her copy machine with it. She's not happy about it."

"What do you think?" asked James as Genevieve put on a thick pair of reading glasses.

"It looks pretty legit, aside from the inconsistencies in tense agreement maybe, and, The *Bowing Out* intro and last lines are in a much larger scrawl. Like they were written after the original."

Genevieve reverently positioned the copied note on her desk before her, hands placed on either side. She braced herself to read it again. Her mouth moved slightly as she went over every word.

She sighed, "He wasn't suicidal."

"So, you think it's a forgery?" I asked.

Genevieve frowned. "No, these are his words. He definitely wrote them. But the last ones… I don't know."

"Then how can you insist he wasn't suicidal?" I asked.

"Because I know… I knew Donatus. He was happier than he'd been in years. He was excited about making big changes in his life."

"Like divorce." James set down his Diet Coke can.

"Yes, and the only person in his life who insisted Donatus was suicidal was Cherry," Genevieve said.

"So, if you don't think it was forged, then you think he was forced to write it?"

Genevieve frowned again as she readjusted her glasses and analyzed the note.

"I think it's a collection of bits and pieces from Donatus' musings over the years. I think this is a pastiche of writings stolen from his poems, letters, notebooks, and such. Someone hastily pieced them together to make it look like a suicide note, and then traced them. That or there's a page missing. The letter is all about his relationship to music, until you get to the larger, uneven bottom scrawl. It's almost like an overkill. The whole, *you'll be better off without me, keep moving forward...* it's all so stereotypical, almost as if whoever added it wanted to make certain no one could miss what it was.

"Cherry called Synroc from my office before Donatus was found. I heard Cherry tell Synroc to make sure you checked the greenhouse. Synroc avoided taking you to it because I'm sure he had a good guess of what you two were going to find." She looked up from the letter. "I think all the weirdness, with not finding him, and that strange letter from Little Chris has to do with this letter. This pastiche was sloppily cobbled together and somehow has to do with the stall in finding the body."

I recalled our cabin adventure. "Cherry completely forgot she told us she was responsible for the media plant. I've also been seeing a recurring logo; an image of an upright pen balancing scales of justice.

"It's of a pen for sure, with definite scales hanging off of it."

"That would be the Veritas Society," Genevieve said. "They're a sect of Scientology and whatever they're true purpose is, I can't say. I've heard many speculate the Illuminati run the media and Hollywood. I can tell you for certain, as a major league entertainment lawyer, that Cherry now has enough money to be of interest to the Veritas Society.

"It's amazing how she can get away with this. Grieving under the martyrdom of rock star widowhood with her colossal paranoia; half of Hollywood is terrified of her." Genevieve shook her head.

"Let me get this straight." James shifted in his seat, picked up his soda and tapped the top of the can out of habit, then set the empty can back down again. "You're suggesting that Cherry is essentially controlling the media right now."

"She has my team sending out Cease and Desist letters like they're Chinese take-out menus. Right now, she has control over all Bliss P.R. The other band members are lawyering up. She's been hiring private detectives to intimidate Donatus' friends say they won't speak to the press. It's the classic, most transparent intimidation tactic; she's had almost a hundred people interviewed by now. It costs quite a bit of money to have so many people interviewed at length, Cherry's sending a message. I believe all the weirdness has to do with the suicide note."

"I've caught wind of some of that too," I said.

Genevieve nodded her head. "She's in a very powerful position, and she knows it."

"Well, if there's an entire industry guarding her, no one will even talk to us now. At least we're still getting paid. Cherry is clearly going to get what she wants." James eyed me sideways, his slightly pointed chin and sturdy jaw line jutted out. "Brittany, I know that look. What's on your mind?"

I looked up at Genevieve's wall of credentials. UCLA undergraduate degree in political science, a master's degree in feminine studies from Stanford, and a law degree from Yale. Ultimately, her degree was in overachieving.

"I want to know the truth. That's all my job requires in its most basic description. Finding the truth."

"You, know. I do know someone who might be willing to help you." Genevieve leaned in and crossed her fingers. A few strands of hair fell out of her perfect bun. "But you can't ever let it get back to Cherry that I told you. They're not the most reliable sources of information, but they're not afraid of Cherry."

"We're listening." I took out a pad and pen.

"This sounds ridiculous, but they're like the special forces of paparazzi. You can hire them for a "photographic hit," no joke, and no movie star or celebrity is off limits, for the right price. I've sued them multiple times. I even orchestrated a payoff for photos of Cherry drunk and –to put it mildly- indecently exposed."

Genevieve opened a desk drawer, tool out a ledger and a note pad and began scribbling. "You can contact them at this number. They wear disguises, and prefer to meet in some loud area underneath the LAX flight path. When Cherry sent her thugs after them for writing about her and Donatus' heroin use they laughed them off their backs. Cherry really hates them."

"Why are you sending us to them? What makes you think they'll talk to us?" I asked.

With eyes expressionless and cool, Genevieve sat back in her seat and gave us both a plastered, practiced smile. "They claim to know a man to whom Cherry offered $160,000 to murder Donatus."

I scooped up the piece of paper she set in front of James and me, analyzing the phone number and the names - Jim Bob and Billy Joe.

"Cute."

"Well, wait until you meet them," Genevieve said.

"Sounds like a lead to me." James stood.

"How do we know we're not going to get fired for going down a path our client would forbid?" I asked James.

Genevieve laughed. "You'll know you've hit a soft spot when she keeps retaining your services to keep you distracted. People like Cherry control with money, and briefcase bullies like me."

"So, why are you helping us?" James asked.

Genevieve shrugged, "Donatus was my client, too."

"Thank you, Genevieve," I said.

"Don't thank me yet. Take care."

As we gave our ticket to the parking lot attendant, James touched my shoulder. "I say we head to the office and try to line up this meeting ASAP."

"That's exactly what we're going to do." I said.

At the office, James played with the coffee maker as I began to dial. The first number went straight to a voicemail beep. Hoping it was the beep of a working machine minus a greeting I talked fast.

"This message is for either Jim Bob or Billy Joe. This is Private Investigator Brittany Wolfe of Stacks

Private Investigators and I would like to set up an appointment to meet with you. My number is 682-2759. I look forward… - beep! Shit." I tried the next number. Something horrible and loud that sounded like a fax machine picked up. I tried the next number on Genevieve's list. The same distortion quickly followed the dial tone.

"No luck?" James called from the kitchen.

"No. Damn it."

James walked in with two full mugs and handed me mine. The phone rang.

"Sales call, what do you want to bet?" I lifted the receiver. "Stacks Private Investigators."

The loud sound of someone crunching a snack like chips or nuts reverberated from the other end. "Who am I talking to?" demanded the man between crunches.

"Brittany Wolfe."

"This is Jim Bob. Is this the same Brittany Wolfe working for Cherry Starlet?"

"Yes. I just left a message."

"I never answer my phone."

"Would you be willing to meet with my partner and me?" I asked.

"How did you get this number? Cherry knows throwing money and muscle at us doesn't work with this gig."

"Cherry didn't give it to me. I got it from her lawyer."

There was a pause. "Meet us tomorrow, noon, at the Shell Station just off the 405. La Tierra Boulevard exit

141

heading south. We don't have time for bullshit. If you're late we're taking off."

"OK. What kind of car will you be in?" I asked, but Jim Bob had already hung up.

"They agreed to meet with us," I told James.

"Alright, but what does that mean exactly?"

"I need to run an errand real fast." I gathered up my things.

James' blue eyes narrowed. "You're not meeting them right now, are you?"

"Of course not. I'll be back in about an hour."

17

Excitement pulsed through me as I pulled the
Impala out of the parking garage. If I remembered
correctly, Ryan's routine kept him at his home office
Monday through Wednesday. I needed to be honest
with myself. I was just in need of some guidance; this
wasn't an excuse just to see Ryan Kemp. Or was it?
Ryan's fame was more of a turn off than turn on. Still,
it was nice to feel wanted. I thought back to Donatus'
letter: *Forever in your orbit - Donatus Sun*. That was an
ending, clearly. Then it went on to speak of Cherry
and their child. He could have gotten high, been
coaxed to write a goodbye letter, as opposed to a
suicide note, to his fans, then was shot up with more
heroin than he wanted. I needed a copy of the autopsy
report.

I drove to the northwestern edge of Wilshire
Boulevard just north of the Santa Monica pier. I
lucked out finding parking. A few bicyclists in shorts
and bikini tops rode by on their beach cruisers. I rang
the doorbell, then looked up and waved at the camera.
It took a few minutes for the two-sided glass door to

143

open.

"Brittany, hi. What's up?" Ryan held a coffee mug, the wrinkles around his eyes standing out more prominently as he smiled. He wore only blue and white Hawaiian board shorts and a blue pen behind his ear. His tussled hair completed the sun worshipper look. Light shaded freckles were beginning to show on his shoulders and biceps.

"Hi, Ryan. Sorry to bother you, but I have some questions. I'm doing research on the Donatus Sun case and can use your media insights, particularly lower media. Cynthia isn't here, is she?" I peered over Ryan's tan shoulder.

"No, she's in Paris for Fashion Week with bimbo friends hooking up with their man-bimbo hangers-on. How low is the media we're talking about?"

"Bottom feeder low."

Ryan gestured me inside. I followed him toward the back kitchen through the blonde wood and glass paneled home. His LA bachelor pad beach house was set up for entertaining. A giant sliding door led out to a tri-level infinity pool, the top level feeding into the bottom one. At the very top a stone Jacuzzi tub had a miniature stream warming the mid-level pool while Ryan and his guests looked out over the Pacific toward Malibu.

"Have you heard of the Stalkerazzi?" I asked.

Ryan's eyes narrowed as he sipped his coffee. "You weren't kidding. What are you getting involved with them for? They're known for some shady shit."

"I was told they might have some information I

need. And they're not afraid of the Veritas Society."

"Look Brittany, the Stalkerazzi brothers deal with violent drug dealers and low-level pimps, but the Veritas Society? How do you know them?"

"You know who they are?"

"They're scary as shit." Ryan's eyes grew wide as he looked around the counter for his beverage, then picked it up with his hand trembling.

"You're scared of a weird cult? You, the writer who has demons in his sleep?"

"I'd rather battle the legion than the Veritas Society," Ryan said taking a drink.

"Getting back to my original question. You know the Stalkerazzi brothers?"

"Of course I do. They're the pariahs of Hollywood. Parasites of journalism. They pride themselves on derailing careers. Remember when the British actor Thomas Theriot got busted receiving a blow-job from a high-end prostitute in his car parked along the Sunset Strip?"

"Yes, of course." I nodded.

"Well, that was them! They set up T.T."

I looked at him with sideways confusion.

"Thomas Theriot. They set him up with a prostitute named Devine from their pimp friend Ross. Thomas gets caught, then goes from making five million a picture to a pariah, then owing a shit ton in alimony to his super model, now ex-wife."

"I have a meeting with them tomorrow," I said.

"You've already contacted them? All I've heard of them lately was when Donatus Sun and Toyland's bassist Kristie White were together, Cherry threw her weight around and the bidding for the pictured evidence got canceled. Although, I'm sure they'll find a buyer for those prints eventually. Like, no tabloid or anyone from the Associated Press was willing to break the story. She must have already been backed by the Veritas Society. It's all real scary shit."

The doorbell rang. As Ryan left to go answer it, I closed my eyes to listen to the trickling of the man-made backyard waterfalls.

As I took in the new guest following Ryan back in my heart pounded in my throat. James' blue eyes glared at me. What was going on? James' colossal vanity didn't allow for situations like this.

"What are you doing here? You followed me," I said through clenched teeth.

"I thought you were meeting the Stalkerazzi without me. For all knew they insisted you meet with them alone, and you're just crazy enough to. Remember the homeless guy from skid row who proclaimed he was the "Grandson of the Son of Sam?" Your whole excuse of, *I felt safe because he only murders brunettes* crap?"

"I came here because Ryan knows about the Stalkerazzi guys."

"You really shouldn't meet them alone. These guys are not female friendly," Ryan said. Every muscle in his jaw was clenched. I stepped away, as if ignoring them both would prevent violence between them.

James removed his hands from the pockets of his light leather jacket. "Don't worry, she won't. Brittany, I'll talk to you back at the office. You know better than to make a move without me, honey." James let himself out. He never called me honey. He walked out slowly in that intense way a man does when he is willing a fight. It felt like ages for the front door to open and shut.

"That's the new boyfriend?" Ryan asked.

"It's complicated."

"I miss you, Brittany."

Ryan set down his coffee mug, and reached for my waist. I pulled away.

"Really?" he asked.

"I need to go, Ryan."

Ryan walked with me to the door. "Can I call you, OK?"

"Sure." I let Ryan kiss me, but briefly.

As I walked back to my car, Ryan called after me. "Brit, you know you can call me at any time."

"Yeah, I know."

When I arrived back at the office I was relieved to see James' motorcycle in the parking lot.

"Hi, I'm back," I announced.

"Hey." James was sitting at the desk hanging up the phone. "We need to talk."

#

Back in the Valley, I took Alpha on a three-mile run. After a shower and a glass of wine, I lit some aromatherapy candles advertised to help you decompress. I took a few uppers, then lit them up. After drinking a few mellow cocktails, I regained my hunger. I found some noodles and sauce in the back of one of my pantry shelves and put a bowl of dog food on the kitchen floor for Alpha. I sat down on the edge of my bed with the lit candles on my dresser top, and my ten-minute pasta in my lap, I luxuriated in being off my feet and able to eat without my stomach tied in knots.

Laying back I let my mind bounce around. I imagined owning my own private investigators firm, Wolfe Investigations. I thought of what my perfect relationship looked like. I couldn't take someone else's last name. The man's name being a better detective name than Wolfe would be highly unlikely. After a few minutes of meditating I managed to focus on one clear desire without question. These kids, these Donatus Sun followers, needed to stop killing themselves. If I could just prove he was murdered, the copycat suicides would stop.

I blew out my candles and ate my pasta in front of the TV in the living room while Alpha moved her soggy chicken flavored chewy next to me. I flipped through follow up reports on Cherry Starlet and the death of Donatus Sun and now her bassist Kristie White. In one interview, Cherry tearfully recalled Kristie White's life, announcing they were close like sisters.

"I should have known," she sobbed. "Just like Donatus' mom knew to call the cops after he purchased that God-awful gun. For the record, I was not in the hospital that night. I have witnesses who were at my hotel and can attest to it. The press is lying about me and I can prove it. Don't lie!"

Genevieve was right. It was amazing how Cherry could get away with this. The media was simply a bunch of stage puppets reiterating her lies, while she gleefully wiggled her fingers.

I yearned for the bottle of chardonnay in the fridge, and two fingers and a very generous thumb of the scotch in my cabinet, but not tonight. I knew I needed all my brain cells for full use tomorrow morning.

While I tried to fell asleep listening to Alpha's rhythmic snoring, I couldn't stop wondering what errands James had to do earlier. Why had I agreed not to go anywhere without James for the rest of the case? Guilt? I thought about the cold bottle of wine still corked in the fridge. I got up and went to the bathroom medicine cabinet and took a sleep aid.

18

It was 6 a.m. when my alarm went off. I was already wide awake. I hopped out of bed and switched it off. Alpha lifted her head up briefly, gave me the stink eye, and laid her head back down with a *harrumph*. After two cups of coffee I was full of nervous energy, my hands quivered with anticipation as I took Alpha, disgruntled, on her early walk and poured her breakfast.

I tried to clear my head on my run. Donatus alive was worth a Columbian drug stash. Donatus dead was worth a fucking fortune. This case wasn't like anything I'd ever done before. Standard P.I. work typically required mind-numbing patience. You have to sit and watch a door for six grueling hours, maybe longer. You know your guy is inside, and you can't leave until he does. Don't lose him, it was that straight forward. You can't get up to use the bathroom or get a cup of coffee. You can't have any gaps. Grueling or not, I missed it. In this case, nothing was straight forward.

After blow-drying my hair, I scooped it up in a

ponytail and put on a San Francisco Giants baseball cap, cover-up, mascara, and I was out the door.

James wasn't just on time, he was early.

"You ready to roll out?" James asked.

I checked my satchel for my tape recorder and Polaroid camera, then stuffed a legal pad and some pens in my briefcase. That's when I noticed a large metal briefcase leaning against the desk.

"What's that?"

"That is the Bacharach True Pointe 1100," James said.

"Holy crap. Where did you score a portable lie detector?"

"Rick's."

"The P.I. in West Hollywood?"

"Yup, the same. He owed my Uncle Joe a favor. I found him yesterday. We have to be careful with it."

"What kind of favor?" I asked.

"I'm not at liberty to say."

We loaded up, hit the road, and right at the entrance to the Santa Monica Freeway hit bumper-to-bumper traffic.

"Shit." I tried to secure my latte in between my legs as I rolled down the window.

Coasting on caffeine and a few black beauties, I white knuckled it all the way to La Tierra Boulevard. We were a few minutes late by the time we pulled into the Shell Station parking lot. A dark purple Ford Fiesta containing two men with dark beards, sunglasses, and matching handle bar mustaches pulled up. They "mean mugged" James. We got out of the

Impala and walked toward the ugly clown-sized Fiesta, but before we could get there a red, cherried out late 70s Chevy Monte Carlo cruised around the gas station and pulled up next to our Impala.

Two clean-shaven men sat in the car's black leather seats. The driver rolled down his window. He wore dark sunglasses, a black bandana over his blond hair. His friend looked the same, only his bandana was yellow. Their noses looked a tad off color and strange.

"Brittany Wolfe?"

I nodded. "That's me."

They looked at James.

"I'm James, her partner."

The men put the car in park, shut it off, and got out. It was quiet except for the honking from the freeway.

"He's Jim Bob and I'm Billy Joe," said the black bandana. His voice was nasal.

"Isn't Billy Joe a girl's name? Guessing those aren't your actual names," James said.

"Nothing gets by you," Jim Bob said as he adjusted his yellow bandana. His voice was also strangely nasal. In the direct sunlight, I realized what was so strange about their noses. They were both wearing high quality prosthetics; I was impressed by their serious disguises.

James bristled. "We were told that you know a guy who claims Cherry Starlet tried to hire him to kill Donatus Sun."

"Yeah. We know him well. He's…" A large low flying Boeing jet flew overhead blaring us with the roar of its dual jet engines. As James and I covered our ears the men began laughing.

"Come again?" James asked.

"What? You didn't get that?" Billy Joe said.

"Do you have information or not?" James looked back at the Impala.

"His name's Tapatio. He's the lead singer of the band Los Demonos, and he's not easy to get ahold of," said Billy Joe as Jim Bob re-adjusted his yellow bandana.

"Can you take us to him?" James asked.

"That depends. What's it worth to you?"

"Five hundred," I said ignoring the looks James was giving me.

"We don't even get on the 405 for less than fifteen hundred."

"Twelve hundred," James said.

Jim Bob laughed.

"Fifteen hundred," I said. James shot me another look.

"Two grand, and remember, we're the only ones who know where to find this guy. He moves around a lot," Billy Joe said.

"OK. You'll get two grand if and when we find him." I pulled out a pen and notepad. "So, Tapatio of Los Demonos?"

"Yeah," Billy Joe said. "He claims Cherry Starlet offered him $160,000 to kill Donatus. The last I heard he lives out in Riverside, but it's hard to say. He moves around, but we know how to track him down."

"Can he meet us here in West LA?" James asked.

"No, he avoids coming into Los Angeles proper.

When he's here for shows and promotional work he almost always gets hassled by the cops. You aren't police, are you?"

"No," James said quickly shooting me a look.

"Good. Los Demonos used to open for Red Erickson's band Robotic Tension until Tapatio's shows grew to be too extreme. Red Erikson was the one to introduce Cherry to Tapatio. If Cherry really wanted someone killed she'd know Tapatio would do it or find someone to do it." Billy Joe snapped his fingers, "Like that."

I tried to imagine a Latino man naming himself after a hot sauce. It wasn't jiving with me.

"Why do the cops hassle him?" I asked.

"You got to understand, parents of the kids who are fans of Los Demonos absolutely hate this guy. He's a debaucherous man, and is heavily into Southern California's kink scene. He wears an executioner's mask and has young women perform sex acts with him on stage. The last album he released was called *Satan's Sex Slave*."

Gross. "So, how do we find him?"

"Do you have time to follow us?" Billy Joe motioned to Jim Bob, and they got back in their car.

"What are you thinking?" James asked me.

"Yeah, we'll follow you." Back in the car I patted James' leg. "We're going to need that lie detector you scored," I said as I followed the Stalkerazzi out of the parking lot.

We tailed the red Monte Carlo toward Central Los Angeles and into Korea Town, eventually parking in a lot on West Eighth Street and Wilshire.

Once parked, James and I followed Jim Bob and Billy Joe around the corner and into R Bar, a pirate themed karaoke joint so colorful it looked like a few of its stuffed parrots managed to rapidly procreate, then exploded all over the place. It was mid-afternoon. Fruity drinks with umbrellas weren't yet being served. Billy Joe ordered a Diet Coke, and James and Jim Bob declined a beverage. I had a beer.

"A few of Tapatio's friends buzz around here daily. Those bar flies will usually give up all kinds of information to get us to buy them another round of drinks, but I'm not seeing any of them here today." Jim Bob scratched underneath his yellow bandana.

"I see someone who might be able to help," Billy Joe said as he began walking toward a young, beautiful, blue-eyed black woman aggressively dressed for the afternoon. She had on a bright yellow minidress and white high-heeled pumps. She smiled wide as Billy Joe approached her and the two hugged. Billy Joe must have said something clever to make the woman laugh. I observed the adult version of Disney's *Pirates of the Caribbean* for a few more minutes before the couple came walking back toward us.

"Monroe Divine, meet Brittany and James. You already know my brother Jim."

So, they were brothers, or that was the story they were sticking to. Monroe hugged Jim Bob, then shook both our hands.

"Nice to meet you."

"Monroe's old man, Ross Cagney, had just seen

Tapatio, and he'll be able to take us to him."

Monroe downed the rest of her little glass of wine. We exited and walked around the corner together, and I let James take my car keys. I wanted to set up my tape recorder and check my notes. We followed the loud, shiny red car to the front of the Wyndham Hotel where they let Monroe Devine out. James put the Impala in park and got out to speak to the Stalkerazzi men, then got back in the driver's side of the idling car.

"Monroe's getting her pimp, and we're following them out east," James said.

"Pimp? Is that what they said?" I asked.

"They didn't have to. Don't you recognize her? She's got to be the most popular hooker on the LA sex for sale circuit. Her face has been splashed all over the tabloids for weeks."

Her face and those of movie stars had been staring at me in grocery checkout lines for weeks. Ryan had even mentioned it. She's the one who got caught blowing that movie star in his car on the strip. It ruined his marriage and his career. Her popularity must be outstanding. The Stalkerazzi really played the media well. It was a story with the intoxicating aroma of rebellion, followed by the stench of guilt. They must have made a fortune.

Monroe Devine came slinking out of the hotel on the arm of a finely dressed black man wearing a gold Rolex, an understated gold pinky ring, black suit, and fashionably long dreadlocks. Once they climbed in the back of the red Monte Carlo, we were off.

They drove fast, but no speed the Impala couldn't

keep up with. Plus, it's hard to lose sight of a bright red muscle car. We drove for about an hour through the half desert, half chaparral plains of Pomona and Ontario.

"And, we're into Riverside," James said as the town's sign loomed over the exit as we followed the red car.

After a few turns the streets became uneven gravel and dirt with tall green trees sparsely placed, looming over what looked like the entrance to a piece of large property. We soon came upon a long ranch house with peeling yellow paint. From afar it looked like it could be a giant trailer. Behind the pre-fab, manufactured house was a large yard, its boundary set with a white picket fence. In the front was a large, red, fenced-in chicken coop. Miniature goats roamed the backyard. It wasn't a place I could imagine Monroe Devine, her pimp, or any musician hanging out.

I looked over at James as we stopped. "Where the hell are we?"

19

We got out of the car and approached the Chevy. Devine's pimp, Ross, was the first one out of the shiny red car.

"You coming, Monroe?"

"Hell, no."

Ross walked up to us. His smile was wide and full of white teeth, with the exemption of a gold capped canine. His mouth looked happy, but his eyes told a different story.

"Jim Bob and Billy Joe says you guys are cool. You're not police?" Ross' eyes narrowed. He tossed his dreads over his shoulders and flexed threateningly.

"Neither of them are law enforcement, Ross. I'd have smelled it on them," Billy Joe said.

James and I followed the three men past the clucking of chickens, around back, and up to the seven to eight-foot-high white picket fence.

"There he is. Hey man. It's Ross."

"Who else is with you?" asked a man's voice through the screen door.

"Some people want to talk to you about Cherry

Starlet."

"OK," said the dark figure through the screen.

The screen door opened and a pudgy balding white man with wild red-rimmed eyes wearing a white, wife-beater tank-top and pants that looked like navy blue Dickies leaned outside and squinted at us.

"You're Tapatio?" James asked.

"Yeah. Who the hell are you? I already don't like your face." Tapatio said to James, then eyed me up and down. "And look at the goodies you brought with ya."

His nose, lips, and brows were carved out of his flat stump of a face. His black beetle eyes dove out of sight when he blinked his eyes. I was mostly shocked that he was white and named Tapatio. I wonder if his fans knew. Was he always under an executioner's mask?

"Did Cherry Starlet ask you to kill her husband?" I asked.

"She offered me $160,000 to whack Donatus Sun, I just didn't think she was serious. When she's all strung out on dope the woman's all over the place. When she offered me that money, damn I wish I'd have taken it. I know who killed him though. Son of a bitch tried muscling me into shutting up about it too, so screw it, I'm not covering for the bastard. The FBI can catch him for all I care."

"We brought a lie detector with us. Would you be willing to take it and sign off on the paperwork while we tape record it?" James asked.

Jim Bob's and Billy Joe's mouths dropped open underneath their prosthetic noses. Ross and Tapatio started laughing.

"Only if your broad shows me her tits first," Tapatio said to me.

I turned around and began walking back to the Impala.

"We'll pass," James said.

"Alright, wait. I'll do it. I'll sign it and everything. I'm happy to call out that bitch. Come on, put me in the news! I can't stand the woman," Tapatio said.

I had a hard time imagining Tapatio liking any woman. After getting the lie detector out of the trunk, we set up in Tapatio's living room. The place looked like it had been put together by leftovers from a flea market's aftermath. I was surprised to see shelves of books. I did a brief skim and picked out Charles Bukowski's, *Love is a Dog from Hell* and Joseph Conrad's, *Heart of Darkness*.

I could see through the window on the side of the house and into the open door of a work shed. Guitars were propped up on stands. A chainsaw and circular saw laid on a workbench. With all the sharp tools displayed prominently in the open shed, and all the wires and electrodes being attached by James to Tapatio's head, fingers, and forearms, it was Rob Zombie's house meets *The Texas Chainsaw Massacre*.

"What are you two staring at? You better not be taking pictures or recording me." Tapatio growled at the Stalkerazzi. "You know I hate that shit."

"Shit Tapatio, those boys would stick their heads in fire if we told them they could see hell," Ross laughed.

"Alright, we're ready. Let's start with a few test questions. What's the name of your band?" James held a notepad while observing the machine.

"Los Demonos," Tapatio said.

"Good. When was your last drink?" James said.

"Last night, I don't know, around 2 a.m. maybe."

James observed the needles bouncing up and down on the scanner and notated some lights on the machine.

"OK, now tell the truth."

"About half an hour before you guys got here. Damn, this machine's good." The other three men laughed.

Once we got through all the questions, including, "Did you kill Donatus Sun?" and "Do you know who did?" we packed up. I couldn't wait to leave. The whole property gave me the creeps. As we left it felt like someone was watching us. I kept looking toward the cluster of trees. Monroe Divine straightened out her yellow minidress as we approached. She leaned against the car and observed us.

"He's telling the truth," James said.

"Are you sure?" I asked.

"I've tested hundreds of people while paying my dues in the district attorney's office. When I asked if Cherry Starlet offered him money to kill Donatus Sun it registered a 99.9; he's not lying."

"But, if he's a sociopath he can pass it, right? It's possible?" I asked.

"Yes, it's possible, but not likely," James said.

When we got back to the office, I reorganized the trunk of my car. James took out the lie detector, and I shifted some file boxes filled with old case work I needed to go through at home. I liked to watch television while shedding paper. James came back out.

"Hey, what's up?" I asked him.

He was already putting on his bike helmet. "Something came up, and I've got to take off."

"Take off to where?"

James kept walking. "James, what's wrong?"

But his motorcycle was already roaring out of the parking lot. I went inside to check the office answering machine, and on my desk was a bouquet of red roses. My heart pounded, sinking down into my stomach. They were beautiful. Shit. The card attached to the stick was written in bold, red letters.

Being with you reminds me of what I'm missing. Dinner? – Ryan

I tried calling James, even though I knew he wouldn't answer. Back at home I walked Alpha, drank a bottle of wine way too fast, and went to bed.

20

The next morning, I sat in bed with Alpha re-reading Dante's *Inferno's* eighth and ninth cantos. In a daze, I made a pot of coffee, then drank a cup of it while flipping through my coffee table book of Rodin's *The Gates of Hell*. Its naked, muscular descent into complete misery and total despair - it gave me a peace. I thought of Dante's view of what it means to be in Hell. It's a collapsed imagination. Cherry was in front of Donatus standing on a media platform of lies. Hell was not allowing the fullness of what was really there be seen. Tapatio was there, the Stalkerazzi where there. The notion that we look and we see what's really there is naïve realism. I tried to reach James again, hoping that maybe he'd pick up.

I crawled back into bed with my coffee and reread my favorite parts of Dante's *Devine Comedy*. His character, the tragic and beautiful Beatrice, took care of me. Soon I was caffeinated to the point that I had no choice but to get up. I put on my running gear and clipped Alpha into her leash. She needed no convincing.

As we ran my mind went to James. Are all East Coast prep school boys such big babies? He was constantly reminded by his girlfriends of what a great catch he was for going to high school in Switzerland, for completing a triple major in political science, history, and geography. He graduated law school young and had a rotation of attractive women and a heavy partying lifestyle. He was the youngest man to make partner at a large firm. Now he was sober, a P.I. working for his uncle's company. He saw my reconnecting with Ryan as a rejection; something he'd never had to deal with before. He was like a petulant child.

By the time we made it back home Alpha and I were both panting hard. My lungs were burning. My heart was in my throat surrounded by the acrid taste of bile. I laid down on my cool kitchen tile and listened to Alpha lap up water from her bowl near my head.

After my body cooled down I got up and made myself some toast. I wasn't hungry. I was a little thirsty, and my stomach knot was loosening. After a long shower the runner's high was gone. I moped around until 6:00 and opened another bottle of wine.

Damn neighbors were throwing a party. Twice in the night Alpha woke me up with her growling. The next morning I sat up in bed with a dull headache. Alpha was whining at the front door.

"Alpha. Just go out back. Go out your doggy door."

After I took some Advil and slugged down a hot cup of coffee, Alpha was still scratching at the front door.

"Alright. Jeeze." I grabbed her leash and we went out front.

Alpha ran over toward the car. It was a muggy and overcast day. The sight of the Impala sent a chill over my body. All four tires were deflated, hacked, and slashed causing its body to rest on its rims.

I went back inside, my heart pounding. I tried to call James. No answer. Damn him and his caller I.D. Grabbing a phone book cursing, I called my friend's auto body shop in Encino; I was using the term friend loosely. When my dad was still alive, I met Eddy at a car show. We went out to dinner, then had one of the best bedroom romps ever. He wasn't that bright, but he was very good looking. Eddy barely got any of my jokes, but I dated him for months for his physical talents.

"Yeah, Eddy. Slashed. I'm going to need a flatbed tow. When can you scoop me up?"

"I can send someone in an hour. How have you been?"

After 20 minutes of baseball and small talk the tow truck was on order. I took Alpha for her walk, trying not to look at my car. When I eyed the Impala my rage picked back up. Its heavy body was too much for its rims. I remember my father's face when he finally found the perfect wheels, which are probably going to have to be replaced. Looking at it now, it was like someone broke the legs of a family member.

I tried to distract myself with paperwork. This only worked for a few hours before my mind snapped back to James who had just attacked my car. I took Alpha for another walk. When we got back my phone was ringing. I ran to answer it. Maybe it was James!

"Hello?"

"Genevieve's really freaked out that you mentioned her name to the press." Cherry exhaled heavily on the other line.

"Excuse me?"

"Why did you contact Tapatio, and who the hell said you could talk to the fucking tabloids?"

"I don't know. What are you talking about, Cherry?"

"It's all over the news! You've linked my name to a psychotic pervert!" There was that famous temper, and the timing couldn't be worse with my mood souring by the second.

"Cherry, if you don't like how we're handling the investigation than just fire us," I said.

"No. No, that's not what I want," Cherry's voice grew louder.

"I don't know what you've heard. I haven't spoken to the press, but James and I have done some investigating. Didn't you say you wanted the truth, no matter what the cost?"

"Yes, I know. Just report to me before you go out and interview people. I'm paying you to keep me in the loop. Don't talk to that lying madman again. You should be focused on what my nanny, Little Chris might know. Just get back up to Seattle and come to the house. He's here now. The baby is with Brianne, Donatus' mom, but I'll make Little Chris sit tight until you get here. Do you think you can get up here in the next few days?"

"I don't know. Let me see," I said trying to flip through my mental appointment Rolodex. I shuffled through my things for my calendar.

"What am I paying you for? You work around my schedule, not the other way around. You work for me!" Cherry yelled. I had to move the receiver away from my face as the earpiece vibrated.

"I won't be for much longer if you don't cool down and begin talking to me. I demand some respect."

"What the hell does that mean?" Cherry asked.

"Talking. You know, it's like yelling only not as loud."

Cherry audibly took in a deep breath, and exhaled. "Look, I could technically go after your license, but I would never do it. I think you're a great P.I., and we women..."

I couldn't stand her voice another second. "I'll let you know when I can get back up to Seattle."

"I'll pay you when you get here, and..."

I plunked down the phone. "Someone slashed my tires by the way," I said to no one.

My car wouldn't get to the shop until after Eddy closed. I was stuck. I looked for Sgt. McNeil's phone number. Alerting the Seattle Police Department to the new lead was the least I could do.

"McNeil speaking."

"Sgt. McNeil, this is Brittany Wolfe calling from LA."

"Who?"

"I'm the private investigator who was hired by Cherry Starlet."

There was a heavy sigh on the other line.

"There's a man down here in LA who claims he was solicited by my client to kill her husband. He's the lead singer of a heavy metal band here in LA, and I spoke with him. He passed a lie detector test. You really should look into it."

"Look, these kinds of cases cause all sorts of attention grabbing yahoos to pop up. We received a phone call last week that someone had proof Donatus was still alive, like he was Elvis or something. It's ridiculous. We've already done a complete investigation. Nothing has indicated this case is anything but a suicide."

"You didn't even develop the film from the crime scene," I said carefully to keep the anger out of my voice.

"We usually don't even arrive on the scene for suicides. If the patrol officer feels confident it's a suicide, the ambulance and coroner are the only services required to show."

I was astounded. "You would let a patrol officer, with no homicide experience call whether it's a suicide or not? Are you serious?"

"I called it, OK. I was at the scene, and I have plenty of experience. Nothing about this case is changing that call, especially the musings of a lady P.I. hired to find the man and failed to locate him dead in his own home!" The phone slammed in my ear.

I called to set up my flight, grabbed the bottle of whisky out of the cabinet, a dog-eared paperback, *The Postman Always Rings Twice*, and plopped down on the couch next to Alpha. My wheels were gone, my client was unhappy, and my boyfriend was mad at me, but I had my dog. I turned on the radio to Cherry's raspy voice, then turned it off. Toyland's new album had officially skyrocketed. After getting up once to talk to the tow truck driver I spent the rest of the evening reading and watching reruns.

#

I was being chased by a motorcycle. Its bright headlight kept getting closer and closer as I tried to run from it. I tried to jump out of the way, but it was already on top of me.

A motorcycle engine was idling nearby. I opened my eyes and sank down into my bed. It was morning and Alpha was whining and scratching at the door. James! I jumped up and ran to the bathroom to look over my hair and face. After examining my whisky covered tongue I started scrubbing my mouth out with spearmint toothpaste with my stiff bristled toothbrush. My hair hadn't been washed in a few days. I sprinkled my roots with baby powder and ran a brush through it, then grabbed the leave-in conditioner from under the sink and sprayed the ends. I stayed in my barely there see-through pajama pants and white tank top. I covered my chest with an arm as I opened the door, half to protect from the cold and half because the shirt leaves little to the imagination. He'd been an asshole, and he didn't get to see what he'd been missing.

"James?"

A large red-headed, red-bearded man took off his

helmet and dismounted his old black, yellow, and brown 70s Triumph.

"Holy shit!" I stumbled backward into the doorway as he silently approached me. His blue eyes had that thousand-yard stare I was all too familiar with. Every fiber of my being was screaming for me to run. Alarmed by my fear, Alpha reacted with the fearless vigor of a working attack dog. She jumped up and grabbed the man by the sleeve of his jacket with her teeth. I could see the butt of a gun sticking out of his pants.

He's going to shoot her! I rushed back into my house and grabbed my pump-action shotgun from the hall closet and flew back out front with steady posture, my gun aimed.

"You hurt my dog and I'll blow your head off!"

"James!" yelled the ginger-haired man struggling to get Alpha's snarling mouth full of flesh-ripping teeth off him.

I lowered the shotgun and watched James run toward the man from the gate he was trying to shut. James' bike was parked at the end of the tree line.

"Alpha, no!" James shouted.

"Alpha, leave!" I clapped my hands and she halted. By now the man was on his butt. Still on the ground, the redheaded man examined his sleeve. Alpha had ripped through the thick leather jacket. I was relieved there wasn't any blood. As he stood back up Alpha growled.

"Alpha, no. James, what's going on?"

James walked up and gave me a long hug. The smell

of deodorant and his leather jacket filled my nostrils. It was half a minute until he pulled away.

"Brittany, this is my friend, Casey. He moved down here from Alaska and lives close by in Encino. We've fished and hunted together. He's decent with a gun. I wanted to introduce you two so he could come around and check in on you."

"Check in on me?" I tried to imagine my uptight neighbors watching the red-headed biker circling my house.

"Where's the Impala?" James looked around the yard.

"I had to have it towed. Someone slashed my tires. You won't answer my calls for two days, and now you're checking in on me? What the hell has been going on?"

James pulled a rolled tabloid from the back of his pants out from under his jacket, and handed it over. I unrolled it.

"Oh my, God!" There I was on the front cover of *STARS* magazine, walking behind James who was side-by-side with Ross Cagney and Tapatio. The caption read: *Brittany Wolfe, private investigator to the stars sniffs out a confession against her client, Cherry Starlet, from Los Demonos front man Tapatio. Hollywood pimp, Ross Cagney was a part of this unlikely company.*

"We were set up. Billy Joe and Jim Bob, those sons of bitches. They must have made a fortune on the photos and quotes for this article."

I thought back to the eerie feeling I had of someone watching us through the trees. No wonder Cherry was pissed. I was shocked she didn't fire us. She could sue us. Then again, we're on the payroll because it would look worse to fire us. If she fired us after this article, it would make Tapatio's claim appear credible. We were being summoned so she could keep an eye on what we were unearthing in this investigation.

"When Cherry sees this, we're in trouble," James said.

"She already has. She called me yesterday. I've been stranded here, so I had no idea what she was talking about."

James scratched his neck. "Oh, man. We better cash that last check before she cancels it."

"She didn't fire us. She actually wants us to come back up North and talk to her nanny, Little Chris," I said.

Casey and Alpha were making up. His ginger hair almost matched the color of hers. Her ears no longer back, she wagged her tail as the biker patted her head.

"I've got to get going. Good to meet you Brittany, now that your hellhound has decided not to kill me." He scratched her a little behind the ear.

"She's more bark than bite." I motioned her away from the gate.

"I have to disagree." Casey lifted up his jacket sleeve. While there was no broken skin I could see bruises starting to form.

"Sorry about your jacket," James said. "I should have warned you about the dog. I'd never seen Alpha react like that before."

"I'll tell everyone it was from a grizzly up north,"

Casey said.

We shook hands. Casey got on his bike and roared away leaving James and me to stare at each other.

"James, listen..."

"No, hold on. I'm going to ask you just this once, and then I'll drop it because I'm tired of thinking about this asshole. Is there anything going on between you and Ryan Kemp?"

"No," I said.

James breathed a heavy sigh. "Then let's not talk about it again. Have you noticed anything strange aside from your tires? Could it be a reaction to that article somehow?"

"It could be, but someone was messing with my car last week, before the article was published. I could tell they were inside the Impala."

"How?"

"My stereo was turned up full blast. I can think of one person we know that likes to fuck with cars."

James was silent for a moment. Trisha had slashed two of his tires when he had gotten out of rehab in New Jersey. "You think it's Trisha?"

I nodded. "This fits her M.O."

James sighed again. "I'm sorry."

"You don't have to apologize for that psycho. Do you think you can make it up to Seattle with me in a few days?"

"Sure, buy shouldn't we go now, or tomorrow?" James asked.

"I need to give Alpha's sitter some heads up, and I want to get the Impala back and safely parked at the airport while we're gone. Call the travel agent and ask to be put on the same flight as mine," I suggested.

"Alright," James said.

"You want to come inside?" I asked.

"I have to get back to Santa Monica, but listen…"

This was it. Colleagues. I was going work with my former lover and we were going to be awkward and "fake nice" to each other.

"Seeing you with that posturing Hollywood novelist made me want to kill you. Why would you get back with that guy? The one time *The New York Times* even mentioned him it wasn't even about his writing, it was about his car collection. You think I want to see you with anyone, let alone a douche bag like him?" James asked.

Whoa!

"What are you saying exactly?"

"I just want it to be uncomplicated." James turned his head to stare at the wall.

"You're sounding like a pod person. You've never said this before. Are you sure you're OK?"

James frowned and his eyes narrowed. "You never take me seriously."

"Oh, come on. You've never acted serious before."

"I'm different now. I've been clean, Brittany. I need to get going. Pick me up on your way to LAX the day after tomorrow." He leaned in and kissed me on the mouth.

"Are you sure you not dying, or something?" I asked.

James smiled and patted Alpha on the head before

swinging his leg over his Harley. I stared after his black-on-black image as he rode away.

Back inside with Alpha I read and re-read the tabloid featuring me. I was hot news next to the Lisa Marie Presley and Michael Jackson marriage and the amazing batboy. I tried calling Jim Bob and Billy Joe repeatedly leaving messages, but they never picked up or called back. Bastards.

21

It was good to have the Impala back in one piece. I didn't even mind sitting in traffic crawling uphill on the 405.

"I'll never let anyone hurt you again," I said rubbing her steering wheel just like my father would have.

When I picked up James he gave me a big kiss before struggling to get his heavy jacket off in the confines of the bucket passenger seat.

"We'll need to call Cherry from the hotel and ask for an extra day to get over to her lake house. Tell her we have paperwork or something."

"Why?" I asked.

"Because I made an appointment to interview Red Erickson. I don't think we should tip her off since saying that those two are on bad terms is putting it lightly," James said.

"Agreed. James, that's fantastic. Where are we meeting him?"

"He wants us to meet him in his work studio at his house. He said to just cruise over before 6 p.m."

"Nice."

When we landed at Sea-Tac we went to James' car rental place to pick up another black Lincoln Town Car. James handed me a sheet of directions. It had begun to rain hard again. The street signs were almost as hard to make out as James' handwriting.

Down a residential neighborhood street filled with craftsman style homes built in the 50s and 60s we stopped in front of a large, two-story house with a cavernous screened in porch. Once we exited the town car a cacophony of chimes greeted us.

I was surprised how girly the front porch was. Wind chimes hung from little metal hooks screwed into each corner, and Begonias grew out of half a dozen plant pots painted every color of the rainbow. Two metal mailboxes were located on the wall next to the red craftsman style door. One was labeled Red and Sarah Erickson, the other for CRUNCH RECORDS, his record label. Before we could knock, the door opened. The place was shabby chic with a sprinkling of wind chimes and ornate textiles, evidence of a woman's touch. The house of a musician who could live happily as an indie artist and find balance as a family man was hard not to admire.

Stepping out of the doorway, the first thing I noticed about Red was the thin silver chain around his neck held together by a silver safety pin.

"Hey, private investigators to the stars and all that. Come on in," Red said. Standing behind him, a pretty, young brunette held onto a sobbing toddler. "That's my wife, Sarah, and my daughter, Nikki."

"Hi," I said.

"Hello," said the woman bouncing the fussy little strawberry blonde on her hip.

"Follow me. We'll talk in the kitchen," Red said.

He pulled a beer out of the fridge and tried to hand it to James, then me. We both shook our heads, and Red popped it open.

"Thank you for meeting with us and having us over. We understand the precarious position it puts your indie label in considering the power and influence Cherry now has."

"I'm a dad now. When I heard of kids killing themselves it just broke my heart." Red shook his head. "This shit is just unreal. This phenomenon of Donatus Sun fans, Bliss fans, killing themselves. There are fucking suicide cults in Japan canonizing him for fuck sake. Donatus wrote songs that speak to the downtrodden of our society, the misunderstood. They related to him. I've talked to some of the local families whose kids took their lives, and when they read their journals, well, you could see what an influence he was. I don't know. Maybe I can help."

The blonde toddler ran into the kitchen naked and laughing as she was chased by Sarah.

"Hey Nikki-sticky." Red caught the streaker, and handed her back to her mom.

"Let's go down to the studio."

We followed him outside and around to the side of the house where a set of stairs descended into a high windowed basement cellar. Red opened the padlocked door and we all descended after he switched on the light.

"You can play music so loud down here," Red said smacking the walls with the palm of his hand. "These are solid concrete. Each one of these walls is filled with concrete."

The studio was dark, deep, with a ten-foot sound box complete with headset, mic stand, and padded black curtains. The soundboard, computers, and synthesizers were divided by walls of glass. A large drum set and rows of guitars stood prominently in the center divide. Red tugged at a box filled with papers, tapes, and CDs under the soundboard.

"How did you and Cherry meet?" James asked.

"She came to one of my shows and started throwing drinks and ice at me with all her little groupie bitch friends. They were literally grabbing drinks from fans in front of the stage and throwing them at me, heckling me to get off the stage. We, Robotic Tension, were opening for Cherry's loser boyfriend's band. I can't even remember his name or the name of his band, but she was one pushy bitch. After our set she threw a drink in my face, like –pissshh-," Red mimed the thrust with his arm extended, "and started screaming a scathing review in a fake English accent.

"I finally had to hop off stage and threaten her. Security threw her out. Back then they weren't as reluctant to touch women. Then, the very next day she showed up at my room with a bottle of champagne and called it a peace offering. After I poured us each a glass she tried to unzip my pants. No shit. She was glued to me after that. I found out later that her boyfriend dumped her the night before and fucked two of her friends." Red laughed. "I wouldn't even sleep with her for the first six months, but she wouldn't let my ass out of her sight."

"Why do you think she was so obsessed with you?" I asked. Part of me could see Cherry acting on a crazy impulse, then like a Pit Bull refusing to let go. Another part questioned if these weren't the vindictive ramblings of a jilted ex-boyfriend.

"At that time, she thought it was a male dominated world, and if she was going to achieve any fame it would have to be through a man. That woman dressed me, managed me, and nagged me to the point I didn't want to be a rock star anymore. I ran away from it. She wanted me to be what Donatus later became. Thank God, I didn't. I'd probably be dead now, like Donatus."

I looked Red in the eye. "Do you think she killed him?"

"Don't you?" he asked.

Red began pulling out photo books filled with post cards and flyers.

"Donatus was fascinated by artists who died young, and had drug addictions. Jean-Michel Basquiat, Jim Morrison, Janis Joplin, Jimmy Hendrix - he loved them, but he didn't want to join them. Cherry started the whole suicide buzz. I remember her saying to him, *Are you still mad? What are you going to do, kill yourself? Stop acting like such a whiny rock star. You better have taken care of us in your will.* Stuff like that."

Red picked up another journal. A few notebooks

were written in by both Cherry and Red. I read over some of her handwriting. I couldn't tell if it was supposed to be a poem or lyrics.

I'm going to be your wife for the rest of your life.
The death of you and me,
Because it was the start of us...

Creepy.

"Here's one that says Cherry S. That's weird. Her real name is Cherry Mulligan. The name Starlet didn't happen until a few years later. Here's a picture."

Red handed over the photograph. Red, Cherry, a few other celebrities I only knew by face and Donatus all stood arm-in-arm with Red cheers-ing the camera.

"You knew Donatus, well?"

"Yup. Cherry wouldn't even have met him if she hadn't jumped into my bed first. Nobody even knew who Bliss was. When this was taken, she was still with me." He hit a few switches and music began to play. "This is some of Robotic Tension's older tracks."

The sound was upbeat and catchy. The iconoclastic sounds of the late 80s for sure. They were more than good. I could understand Cherry's attraction.

"She did the same thing to Donatus as she did to me. Cherry was always predictably over the top. Her modus operandi was to find out what your peccadillo was and expound on it, but it was never sincere. I'm so glad things turned out the way they did. I make a more than descent living. I'm no teen idol like I was back in the day, but I love my family, and I love my art. If I'd stayed with Cherry I'd be strung out on glam drugs in some sterile mansion like Donatus was."

181

James began to thumb through an aged, dog-eared notebook covered in doodles.

Red shrugged. "All I know is if Donatus wasn't murdered, then he was driven to murdering himself."

On our way to the car, Sarah waved goodbye from the porch, then went back inside.

"Brittany, look," said James.

On the Town Car, shoved under the right windshield wiper was a note written on the back of a plain white envelope.

If you want to know more about C. Starlet, I know someone who can help. 555-2336.

We drove to the nearest payphone and James dialed the number.

"Hello," James said. He was silent for a few seconds, then looked at me and pulled the phone away from his ear. "They hung up."

"Here, let me try." I dialed the number and waited. "Hello, you just left a note on my car?" I cleared my throat, and listened for breathing on the other line.

"Uh, hi," said a woman's small voice. "You were at Red Erickson's?"

"Yes. You left a note on our car saying you have info on Cherry Starlet? How did you know I was there?"

"I recognized you from the tabloids. I was Cherry's and Donatus' nanny. I worked for then up until two weeks before he died."

"OK, listen. Can we come talk to you?"

We arranged to meet at a diner near our hotel, and I hung up.

"This feels a little too convenient," I said as we got

into the car.

When we got to the diner the same *Crimson and Clover* song was playing in the background as when I met with Synroc Landall the first time I was in Seattle. It must be the go-to retro, jukebox request.

James approached a red Formica four-top table where a young woman sat fingering a menu. She was wearing lipstick the color of burnt toast and a long washed out blue, purple, and white floral hippy dress. I recognized her. She looked a bit more mature than her picture with Donatus' daughter on Cherry's nightstand, but it was her.

"Sandy?" James smiled. He looked handsome in his jeans and button-down black shirt. The woman stood up while playing with the sleeves of her fashionable, second-hand looking dress. Sandy was very thin.

"I'm James, and you've spoken with Brittany."

"Hi, Sandy."

"It's nice to meet you." She shook both our hands.

We all sat. The way Sandy played with the ends of her hair made her seem very young. She picked up a menu and put it back down.

"It sucks they don't let you smoke in here anymore," she laughed and began to play with her hair again.

"You were Donatus' and Cherry's nanny?" I asked.

"Yeah, for eight months."

"Why were you let go?" James asked.

"Actually, I quit," She crossed her arms. Her eyes darted from James, me, then back to her fork and knife. It was a bit too soon to start making her defensive. "Cherry wanted to give her friend Little

183

Chris the job, but Donatus wanted me to stay."

"Why did you leave?" I asked.

"I couldn't stand being up there in that big crazy house anymore. It was a good gig in terms of pay, but that was it. They had been through a bunch of nannies before me. That woman was hell to work for. She and Donatus fought constantly," Sandy played with her silverware.

We ordered coffee and Sandy ordered an Oreo milkshake. When our drinks arrived, Sandy played with her straw, stirring her shake in big circles.

"You seem nervous," James said.

She nodded. "I've been scared to talk about this."

"What are you scared of?" I asked.

"Cherry."

I softened my eyes in a way I hoped looked supportive. "Has she threatened you?"

Sandy shook her head and stared down into her milk shake, pulling the straw up and down. "No, but she would, if she knew I was talking."

"Talking about what?" James asked.

"There was a lot of will talk right before I left. Threats like, *You better take care of your girls you bastard.* Shit like that. They were always fighting. When she came home with that custom Mercedes he flipped. It was something you'd see a movie star in. Donatus made her take it back, and then told her he was refusing to play with Bliss at that big music festival. Cherry just completely lost her mind. They had one big blow out, and Donatus locked himself in his workroom. Cherry called the cops saying he was suicidal. He totally wasn't. He had a lot of guns because there had been break ins…"

James put down his chipped, tan coffee mug. "Break ins? What do you mean?"

"Oh, signs of things missing or being moved around. Cherry told Donatus he was paranoid. Then one day I was putting their daughter down for a nap, and I saw a strange man rummaging through the downstairs office. I called the police," Sandy said.

"Any idea who it was?" I asked.

"He took off and was never found. That's when Donatus had a security system installed," Sandy said.

"Do you think when Donatus locked himself in his workroom he was suicidal?"

Sandy shook her head. "No, it was always a joke around the house. Cherry would say anything to get the cops over. When they came Donatus came out of the room and said he was just hiding from his crazy wife. The cops separated and interrogated them in the house. When asked if he had any guns Donatus said no. When they asked Cherry, she said yes. They ended up confiscating them all. Donatus was pissed."

"What do you think Donatus wanted most in those last days?" I asked taking a sip of my lukewarm coffee.

"He wanted to get away."

"From Cherry?" James asked.

"From everything."

"And that's why he committed suicide?" I asked. The only person we'd talked to close to Donatus claiming he was suicidal was still Cherry.

"I'm not sure he did commit suicide." She rubbed

her shoulders and giggled nervously. "I don't know. I can't imagine him leaving his daughter."

"What do you think happened?" James asked.

"I think if he wasn't murdered, he was psychologically pushed into taking his own life, but I really don't know. I overheard Cherry leaving threatening messages on reporters' answering machines, faxing them death threats for reporting her drug use. She'd make recorded threats, and straight up put shit in writing. Cherry always had to be in control."

Cherry's lawyers really were the twelve disciples if she was able to get away with that. James picked up the check, and as we left the diner multiple pairs of feet quickly ran up behind us.

"Brittany? Brittany Wolfe, can you comment on the Donatus Sun investigation? How long ago was it that Cherry Starlet hired you? What are your thoughts on The Sun Men Curse?" A peppy skinny woman in a pantsuit with a sporty blonde bob approached me with a microphone, a camera man, and a sound guy in tow.

Sandy gasped and with her head down covering her face with the back of her hand she ran away clutching her small leather backpack.

"Sun Men Curse?" I asked.

"Yes, how Donatus' great uncle and grandfather both committed suicide."

"I don't know anything about that, and I can't comment on the case at this time,"
I said.

"Have you got anything to say about why you didn't

186

find the body in the greenhouse after he took his life?" asked the excited tiny woman looking from me to the camera man.

"We can't comment at this time," James said as we hurried to get in the Town Car. Camera flashes began going off. I couldn't tell from where.

"Where the hell did they all come from, and how did they know we were here? We should head to Cherry's now. I'd like to get back to LA tomorrow afternoon, and I don't want to give her another chance to stash away Little Chris." I buckled my seat belt as James backed out. People holding cameras jumped out of the way as our surprised faces was captured on film.

When we got to the Lake Washington property I spotted two new media vans parked across the street. The man in the smaller van's driver's side window didn't even attempt to hide the fact that he was spying as he leaned out the window with a long camera lens as we keyed in our password and let ourselves in through the gate.

Cherry had come to the front door, her eyes wide and her red lipstick enhanced mouth. "You two are early. We weren't expecting you until tomorrow."

"We got an earlier flight," James said.

I looked around, craning my neck to view back into the corner of the living room.

"I just had the worst interview on talk radio. The host was no help in defending me from the rude and horrible questions the callers kept coming in with. Camille Paglia has said, *I'm very worried about the low opinion conservative hosts and callers have of the American artist.* They treated me like a scam, a rip-off, a fucking snow job. Fucking conservative elitists."

"Was that this morning?" James asked.

"No, last night, but it went into the morning," Cherry said.

I looked into the study, then walked toward the kitchen. "Is Little Chris here?"

"Yes, I mean, no. He's in Seattle, but he's not here at the house. He went to drop his girlfriend off at her mom's," Cherry said.

"He's not coming back?" James asked.

Cherry checked the corners of her mouth for lipstick by wiping them with her fingers, then studied her fingertips. "He will, but I don't know when. You guys can wait in the living room if you want."

Jenny Lawless poked her head out from the kitchen. Her hair was now a short pixie cut dyed fire engine red.

"Hi."

"Hello," James and I said.

"Jenny and I have some stuff to do upstairs," Cherry said. She squinted at Jenny and motioned with her head to follow her.

As the two women ascended, James and I went into the living room and sat down on the long, deep mocha colored suede couch. James switched on the television and channel surfed. After a few minutes, I thought I heard the front door open and shut. No one came and got us, so I didn't bother getting up. After half an hour, I walked back into the foyer. From there I heard someone in the kitchen.

"Hey, Jenny." I popped my head in to find her digging around in the fridge. "Any word from Chris?"

Jenny leaned out of the fridge door. "Yeah. He's up in the bedroom with Cherry."

"He is? I thought when he got here you guys would get James and me."

"Cherry must have wanted to talk to him first." Jenny shrugged.

Little Chris was supposed to come speak with James and me, not do a pre-interview with Cherry. I reached past her into the fridge and grabbed a Diet Coke. As I popped it open my eyes narrowed at Jenny. Jenny frowned.

"How long have they been up there?" I asked.

"Not long," Jenny said as she crossed her arms.

A few minutes later a door shut, followed by footsteps overhead. Jenny and I walked back out to the foyer and looked on as Cherry and a pale young man with chin length stringy dark hair walked side by side down the stairs. Cherry whispered something to him, and he nodded slowly. His eyes were barely open as his head swayed.

As we entered the living room, James switched off the TV.

"You must be Little Chris. I'm James."

The raven-haired man shook his hand.

"I'm Brittany."

Chris shook my hand as well. We all had a seat. Cherry guided him onto the couch.

"What's wrong with him," James asked.

"Chris has had an exceptionally hard time the last

few days," Cherry said. Next to Chris' relaxed demeanor, Cherry appeared especially tense. Her back was rigid and her eyes wide.

"Do you remember the last time you spoke with Donatus?" James asked.

"Mmmm hmmm, yes," Little Chris said, nodding with his eyes closed.

"Did he come in through the front or the back of the house? Are you sure there was no one else with him that Wednesday morning?" I asked.

"No, no one else was with him," Chris said, looking at us through heavy eyelids.

"Did he come in through the front or the back of the house?" I asked.

"I think it was the front, but it could have been…" Chris' eyes closed halfway, and his head slumped forward. Cherry lit a cigarette and inhaled deeply.

"Whoa buddy. Wake up. What did you just take?" James asked.

Chris opened his eyes a little. You could tell it was a struggle.

"Did you shoot up upstairs just now?" My eyes went from Chris back to James.

Chris didn't say anything. He looked down at his knees, then through his stringy back up at Cherry.

James clasped his hands and leaned in. "Why did you do that when you knew we had to talk to you?"

"I'm fine," Little Chris said.

"No, you're not fine." James gritted his teeth. "Go sleep it off, and we'll see you tomorrow."

Chris nodded, then his head slumped back into his

seat. He looked like he was in a coma.

"Holy shit, he's blasted," Jenny said.

"Yes, he has a lot of problems. He's been real depressed during all of this. I'm trying to get him help. I'm sending him to a rehabilitation clinic in Savannah, Georgia," Cherry said.

"We'll come back tomorrow morning," I assured Cherry.

"You know, I think you might have to do an interview by phone. He's been on a long run and is real sick. I'm going to try to get him on a plane tonight or tomorrow."

Cherry handed the check to James this time. "Thank you for coming up here. I appreciate all your time on this."

She appreciated wasting all our time on this. James looked at the check and raised his eyebrows.

"Also," Cherry handed us some papers, "My attorney, Genevieve, will have a disclaimer for you that I have everyone who works for me sign. This is an abridged version. It just states you won't talk to the press. You'll get the signed portion from Genevieve. If you do it again even without signing she can still go after your P.I. license."

Back at the hotel I went to the bar to be alone with my thoughts while James went upstairs to make phone calls. So much was happening, and it was hard not to be offended that James had one of his biker buddies checking up on me. I was halfway through my third beer when he joined me. Was it the old-fashioned East Coast about him that wanted to check up on me, or old-fashioned jealousy?

"I'm glad you came down. I want to talk to you about something."

"Me first. Trust me. I have a few things to catch you up on."

I set my beer down. "Shoot."

"Donatus' great uncle and grandfather didn't shoot themselves, they both died of freak accidents. His great uncle drunkenly fell down some stairs, and his grandfather died in a freak accident when he dropped his gun in a bar. It was all news spin a la Cherry. The Associated Press is eating her stories up, all she has to do is hold out her hand."

I remembered the articles. "To my complete non-surprise, she's even expounding on her own lies." I picked up my beer. "Now, before I forget, I'm not sure about your biker buddy Casey being my professional Peeping Tom. I know you feel it's your fault Trisha's harassing me, and it is, but enlisting your friend to keep an eye on me is overkill."

"That brings me to the more distressing find I was just about to get to.
Please, no more beer. I want you to listen to me. I talked to Uncle Joe in Jersey, and the word is Trisha's been in jail back east for the last five days. She was arrested for aggravated assault, something about a professor's wife."

I ignored him and downed the rest of my beer. Who's been on my property? Do they have ties to Cherry, Tapatio, or worse? Both?

22

Please make sure your seats are upright and tray tables fastened in preparation for take-off.

"I didn't' mean for Casey to scare you like that, Brittany. I should have called. I wanted to talk to you about the Ryan Kemp tabloid thing. When I saw you at his house I remembered what a douche bag the guy is. I can't ever imagine you going for the literati public health concern now."

My stomach twisted with guilt produced acid.

"What's wrong?"

"I hate it when you're pissed at me, especially when you ignore my phone calls."

"You did the same to me over Vivian."

"Excuse me," I said as a flight attendant walked by. "May I have two Kahlua, please?"

"You know I hate it when you day drink," James said.

"She was wearing my bathrobe at your condo. Now that I think about it, I'm happy you have Casey looking in on me. He's cute, and it'll be nice to have a consistent man around." I glared at him, accepted my liquor from the flight attendant, then leaned against the cabin window. I could ignore him now.

I awoke from a short nap. James had been trying to be nice letting me take the window seat. His arms were folded as he looked straight ahead at the back of the seat in front of him.

"Would you two like anything to drink?" asked a smiling flight attendant with blondish hair.

"No," James said.

"Yes, I'll have a Chardonnay please, or whatever white you have. Thank you." I turned to James. "I'll drop it, if you're serious about this exclusively dating thing. But you know it won't take much for me to doubt your sincerity."

"Just don't end up in bed with a red-headed outlaw biker and I won't do it again." James sighed. "You're not taking anymore go-pills are you?"

"If I do, it'll be your fault." I took a long sip of my wine, and a few minutes later the tension in my shoulders began to relax.

Once James was out I ordered another drink and slept until we landed. The flight attendant hadn't cleared my empties before James woke up.

"Are you sure you're OK to drive?" James pulled my suitcase off the carousal.

"Again, I had two glasses of wine, James."

"Two mini bottles, which is actually four glasses on a three-and-a-half hour flight."

"More like three-and-a-half glasses. I'm fine."

James could be a mean sober. Traffic wasn't bad. Alpha was happy to see me and Anne Marie was

194

happy to take my cash and go home. After taking Alpha on a quick walk I showered in my own tub and got to sleep in my own bed. My two favorite sanctities.

The next day I woke up stuffy. I hoped I hadn't caught anything on the plane. Oh, hell. I was due for a decompression day. I walked Alpha, then stepped into my running shoes and put on a hooded sweatshirt. After pulling my ponytail through a ball cap I set out to do cardio and sweat out whatever bug I had. Around mile three my nasal passageways began to clear, and I was feeling good again. I finished strong. Pulling my ball cap off my sweaty ponytail I opened my gate.

After shutting the gate, I took a few steps into the front yard, and stopped. Music was coming from somewhere. That was odd. I couldn't detect where it was coming from. I took a few steps toward the neighbor's property. Maybe someone had a radio on out by their pool, but the closer I got to the neighbor's property line, the further away the music seemed.

I turned. It was coming from my house. As I walked back toward the driveway I located its exact source. The Impala. *White Rabbit* was playing at a modest level. Had it been on since last night? How was my car not dead? I opened the door and slid inside.

-...*remember, what the door mouse said. Feed your heeeaaad...*-

I turned off the stereo right before the song peaked. I looked at the back seat, then again at the stereo. How was this possible? I couldn't have turned it on and forgot. Taking out my keys that were dangling from the ignition I stood up from my seat. Something was very wrong. My sweat turned cold. OK, stay calm. Where was Alpha? She hated it when I went for a run without her. Usually she was waiting for me at the gate. I stepped out of the car and turn toward my house.

Wham! Something powerful hit me upside the head and I skidded across my driveway gravel on my right elbow, side, and knee. As I tried to figure out what just happened large arms encircled my shoulders from behind. My arms were pinned down to my sides and I was lifted off the ground.

My vision blurred by the blow, I kicked out as hard as I could, sending one of my sneakers sailing through the air.

"Hold still bitch," a deep voice said into my left ear. "It'll be over soon."

My vision was sharp again as I was half dragged, half carried, through my living room toward the bathroom door. I caught a glimpse of Alpha; her big muscular body lay lifeless on the kitchen floor. I screamed and began to kick again.

"Shut up. Shut the fuck up." I felt another blow to my head. I wasn't being hit by anything but his hands. I struggled to remain conscious as I was plunged into cold water. I was being drowned in my own bathtub. I needed to somehow leave my story. I kicked at the faucet and my wall of old serenity blue tile as hard as I could causing them to bend and crack. I wasn't going to be a suicide or a slip and fall. Above the water came a string of garbled curses as he tried to hold my legs down against the rim of the porcelain tub while keeping the rest of my body submerged, his steroided out arm and big meaty hand around my neck holding me down. My chest was on fire and expanding. A high pitch sound was intensifying into a deep low roar. Colors went from red to black.

Somehow, I was able to rise above the waterline. The hands had let go. I still couldn't breathe. After vomiting water, I received just enough air to get my sight back. As the bathroom came into focus I pulled myself out of the tub and dropped to the floor. I was upside down, then right side up. After rolling over lying face down water spewed from my nose and throat. I gagged and choked, gasping for air.

Behind me came a loud crash. I looked up at the eagle-clawed foot of my old porcelain tub, then back at a large crouched man running through the hallway at a thing I couldn't see like a wrestler in a cage match. I watched around the corner as my assailant with a shaved head and handle bar mustache received a swift kick in the face from a black leather boot, then lay motionless. The figure walking toward me took off a leather jacket and had a shock of red hair. His chest heaving, he knelt and I could finally make out Casey's face.

"Brittany, where's your phone. We need to call the police."

"The kitchen," I tried to say, but coughed instead. I couldn't speak. The kitchen. Alpha.

I stood up and staggered towards my dog in the kitchen. Collapsing onto the cold clay tile I could see she had been shot twice and dragged onto the kitchen rug. I put my hands on her midsection and muzzle. A low whimper emanated from her making me blink back tears. I heard Casey walk up behind me.

Then, I felt it. Her chest rose up and down, but slowly. Bits of what looked like raw hamburger meat stuck to the dog door and the kitchen floor.

"She's still alive…"

"Do you have anything to restrain the psycho over… Oh Shit!"

I followed Casey's gaze into the hallway. The man was gone. Two bungee cords were all that was left. I opened the door to the bedroom closet and spun the dial to the small metal safe on the floor. My heart pounding, and still wheezing I opened the safe and grabbed my 9mm and a magazine. After pushing in the clip I shoved in the loaded magazine, chambered a round, then cased the house. The large man was definitely gone.

There was barely any hamburger meat left. I had no way of finding out what Alpha was drugged with. Looking at her in such a prone condition, I could only hope there wouldn't be any long-term damage. She must have lunged at the man before the drugs took effect. That's why he shot her.

C.S.I. dusted for fingerprints, leaving black powder everywhere, coating every door handle and surface in the bathroom. An ambulance arrived a half hour after the cops.

"Are you OK?" Asked a young man, followed by a young woman paramedic. Both were wearing their

198

blue uniform, yellow gloves, and stethoscopes.

"Yeah. Just banged up."

"Let's get you down to the hospital and check you out. You're in shock." The young woman put her hands on her hips as I shook my head.

"No, really. I'm banged up, but I'm OK." I turned to the young man who was checking my heart with his stethoscope on my chest. "Trust me. I was LAPD for years. I've been rattled before. He really wanted to keep it tidy. The man had a gun, but still tried to drown me."

"He tried to fire at me, but the thing jammed," Casey said.

After some arguing, they finally agreed to check me over in the back of the ambulance, and let me go. Minutes after the ambulance left, James rode in.

"Oh, my God." He squeezed me tight. Right then I could feel just how bruised up I was, and I let out a yelp.

James took off his jacket. He was no marshmallow, but even he would have had a tough time with the Jolly Green Giant turned outlaw. I was impressed Casey had subdued him.

"You weren't, he didn't..."

"No. No, he didn't assault me that way." I looked from Casey back to James and winced at the pity pouring out of their faces. Looking down at myself I realized their concern. My wet running outfit clung to me. I had one sock on and no shoes. My hair was half dry and matted to my face. Big ugly bruises were forming on my arms and legs.

"You're sure you don't want to go to the hospital and get checked out? The bruises on your collar bone are getting bigger and darker as we stand here. Shit Brittany, you have an imprint of a hand around your neck."

"James, the cops took Polaroids. I'll take more pictures of myself tomorrow when all my marks are good and dark." I tried to sound unfazed, but my monotone robot voice felt far away as the phone rang.

"They think Alpha's going to make it. It wasn't two gunshots, but a single exit wound through her side. She's coming around from whatever she was dosed with as well. I'll see who I can get to bring her back."

"I thought he killed her," I breathed.

"He only planned to kill you," Casey said. James frowned and turned away.

"Alpha was placed on the rug in preparation to be dumped," James said.

I went back into the bathroom. Even with all my kicking, the seafoam colored mosaic was cracked, but not crumbling. The damage I'd done to the tile and shower knobs was noticeable to me, but would the detectives have noticed?

"You think this had to do with Tapatio and Los Demonos? This smacks of them. Maybe Tapatio decided he didn't want to talk after all." James checked a pager on his belt. That was new.

"It really does. James, you better get some extra security for your condo. You should take my dad's revolver. It's in the safe. You'll probably need to get more bullets."

I got up to go to the safe.

"No, leave it. We got the shotgun and the 9mm. I'm not leaving until this gets sorted out."

I thought for a minute. "I have an idea."

I located Jim Bob and Billy Joe's phone number in the kitchen appliance drawer. After trying Cherry again with no answer, I called the Stalkerazzi. Their answering machine gave a long beep.

"Guys, it's Brittany. We have new information. Whether it's in the tabloids or not, we need to speak with Tapatio again." It was most likely the waist of a phone call, but it didn't hurt to try. Barley a minute later the phone rang.

"Hi, it's Jim Bob." Crunch. Crunch. Crunch. Did the man live on corn nuts?

"Hi."

"What information?"

"What you guys operate on. A pre-packaged sensationalized story ready to sell to the highest bidder."

"You're not bent out of shape because of the little tabloid coverage of you? We did get you a meeting with Tapatio."

If he knew about my attack he wasn't letting on.

"We all have to make a living, some lower than others. We need to get in touch with the executioner again. Can you tell us how to speak with him again?"

"Through a Ouija board," Jim Bob said.

"I'm sorry?"

"Tapatio, real name Maurice Bucket, was found dead near the train tracks close to the Riverside property we visited. It looks like a hit and run done by a large vehicle. That's all we know so far."

I scribbled down the name Maurice Bucket on a nearby notepad.

"I'd leave it alone. It's not safe, but if you do go poking around I wouldn't advertise why you are there. Evidence has a habit of disappearing when people smell trouble."

"I'm picking up what you're laying down," I said.

"Oh, and Cherry is in LA right now. She's the celebrity speaker at an event that'll be attended by A-listers in Century City hosted by the National Civil Liberties Union to boost awareness for First Amendment rights. She's the surprise celebrity guest speaker in defense free speech and the press; the champion of respect for the media."

"You're joking." Hollywood is really willing to look the other way as she punches out writers and threatens esteemed journalists' lives because she's the widow of Donatus Sun?"

"Nope. That lead is on the house. You're welcome."
–click-

Casey and I drank all the beer in the fridge as James downed cup after cup of coffee while we discussed what the Stalkerazzi just shared. The guys insisted on staying the night and I didn't protest. I couldn't bring myself to get back in the tub, but I rinsed off a bit in the sink and put on a fresh pair of sweats.

Alpha was dropped off by what I can only guess was a professional dog walker. She was woozy, and unhappy with the cone on her head to keep her from messing with her stitches. Casey took the couch. Alpha, James, and I were on my California king. I comforted Alpha who lay shivering under the throw I pulled over her. Whatever she was drugged with had a nasty half-life.

23

I awoke the next morning to Alpha licking my face. My sleep was blessedly free of dreams. James was on his side sleeping on top of the covers. After using the bathroom and checking out my bruises I made sure Alpha went outside. She was still shaky but ate some of her food; at least she wasn't trying to lick at her stitches so I didn't have to put that horrible plastic cone back on her head. I made a pot of coffee as the guys woke up.

"Brittany, where did you get this?" Casey walked in from the living room holding Synroc Landall's demo CD.

"Why, have you heard of them?"

Casey shook his head.

"It's from one of Donatus' friends, Synroc. I've only listened to parts of it. It's some kind of hard rock electronica that I've never really been into."

"Take a look at it, again." Casey handed me the CD with the back facing me. Three tracks were listed over a collage of photographs, mostly of men in various stages of performance. The center had a drawing of a hag with pronounced varicose veins. Locksmith, Barber Joe, and Josephine were track titles.

I looked up into Casey's wide blue eyes as I took a gulp of hot coffee. "Yeah, and?"

Casey pointed at a large bald man playing a base, blending into the collage. Even though his image was the size of my pinky finger, I recognized my attacker.

"James, James," I said running into the kitchen. "That's him. That's the man who tried to drown me."

"Are you sure?"

"I'm sure." I was shaking. My heart was pounding.

"I'm positive," Casey said behind me. "If Cherry is trying to shut you up then the best way to get off the – make quiet- list is to go to the press with this right away. Then if you get hit by a car, accidentally overdose on a substance, or even get struck by fucking lightning the public will blame her. She'll pay to make sure no one attacks you again."

"I say we go to the National Civil Liberties Union event tonight. In light of all her recent threats issued to journalists I'm curious to see how she is received as she gives a speech on First Amendment rights," I said.

"That's in four hours and is invite only. The place will be packed full of Hollywood royalty," James said.

"It's the liberal NCLU, and the event is in support of journalism and free speech. We'll go as members of the Associated Press. I have laminated press passes stashed at the office. I bet I could find them. They just might work," I said.

Losing all shame, I quickly showered with the door open taking my clothes off inside the tub. With the curtain closed I toweled off standing inside the claw foot tube I almost died in.

From my closet, I chose a Ralph Lauren white button-down shirt, a black blazer, pencil skirt, and nude pumps. I curled my hair into beach waves. My Fendi clutch was the finishing touch, bought as a gift by my ex-boyfriend so I could blend in at his Hollywood dinner parties.

We ran the Impala through a car wash, and swung by James' condo so the two men could clean up. James' sport coat was a little tight on Casey's broad shoulders, but aside from that the guys looked good.

At the office, James grabbed a small video camera. After some digging I found only one laminated press pass and put it around my neck. It looked legit enough. Back in the car we headed toward Century City. The evening haze was drifting slowly up the canyon ahead, a translucent curtain between the outside world and the privately patrolled world we were about to penetrate.

Cherry Starlet showed up at the Century City Plaza Hotel in her limo in time to open the after-dinner speeches. Valet took the Impala, and once inside the cavernous entryway filled with every walk of celebrity, it was clear to us Cherry was the special guest. We watched as she was greeted by everyone.

Every guest who wasn't press was either in a long formal gown or tux. Flashes went off over some noise in the main hall. Cherry strolled through the hall in a glamorous white satin gown.

Two clean cut men approached and asked her,

"Cherry, what does the NCLU mean to you?" One had a camera, the other a microphone.

"It's like my art, my education. Very liberal. It keeps the American ideal of free speech very much alive, and my family."

The reporter pulled back his microphone and scratched his head. Was he wearing a wig?

"But Cherry, haven't you personally threatened journalists?"

Cherry stood, eyes wide with shock. More cameras flashed around her.

"Have I threatened them? Well, it's my right to defend myself, isn't it? I only take them to court if they lie. Don't lie."

"But what about death threats? We have proof that you've faxed death threats, and left threatening messages ..."

There was something familiar about their voices.

Cherry tried to walk away. "I don't know what you mean. Excuse me."

"What about hiring the front man of Los Demonos to kill Donatus Sun? Was that a joke, or were you serious?"

It was Jim Bob and Billy Joe. Their preppy attire of button-down shirts, slacks, and surfer hair made them unrecognizable. The Stalkerazzi were good! Cherry turned to glare back at the two men. Then, as more cameras kept flashing and light bulbs popped her face morphed back into her coquettish movie star smile.

"Excuse me, hey. Yeah, you two," said a short stalky ring leader of three men in black attire as they stormed up to Jim Bob and Billy Joe. "You need to hand over those cameras and get the fuck out of here."

Pinned on their lapels were gold Veritas Society symbols.

Jim Bob and Billy Joe protested loudly as their equipment was smashed on the ground; the two men were roughly escorted out of sight. The rest of the attendees barely seemed to notice.

I hurried Casey and James inside worried Cherry would spot us and we'd be next. Twenty minutes and a glass and a half of champagne later I saw Cherry walking into the dining area followed by more flashing cameras. Her new image was amazing. James, Casey, and I watched as cameras followed her onto the stage.

"Hi, Brittany." One of the reporters I thought was wearing a wig winked. What a wardrobe change. I could tell even with the new prosthetics the two men who put Cherry on the spot were the Stalkerazzi, aka Jim Bob and Billy Joe. I could see it in their eyes.

We found an empty table to the far right of the stage. A large screen magnified Cherry's image behind her as she stood behind the podium.

"There are so many people in this room tonight who have taught me a lot about integrity, and we live in a time when the Bill of Rights is being attacked, and precious few people are standing up to put a stop to it. All media should feel safe in their First Amendment rights."

I stood up because I couldn't believe what I was hearing.

"Brittany, what are you doing?" James hissed at me.

As Cherry exited center stage right, I walked up to the podium via stage left. The last thing I could see from the crowd as I walked toward the microphone was James and Casey out of their seats right behind me at the bottom of the stairs; they refused to follow me on stage with their mouths agape in horror. As I walked under the bright lights the crowd was pitch black.

"In the interest of free speech, I wanted to ask a few questions. Hollywood has always had a problem distinguishing reality from myth and image, and unless it is considered appropriate behavior to threaten, cajole, and manipulate esteemed journalists, I find it a strange decision on the part of the NCLU to choose Cherry Starlet as a special guest tonight."

The president of the NCLU was already on the stage barreling toward me. The rotund man in a penguin suit pushed his glasses up his nose.

"I don't know who you think you are, but get the fuck off my stage."

My elbow was being grabbed. Two more men who looked like security wearing the same Veritas Society pins were joining him. This clearly wasn't going to be my foray into making after dinner speeches.

As I was escorted out of the party more people came rushing up to me.

"Brittany Wolfe. The detective hired to find Donatus Sun!"

Cameras were flashing all around me. Video cameras were following me. I realized the gravity of my mistake. I couldn't get the cameras out of my face.

I shouldn't have made a move in what isn't my game. I wanted to be anywhere but here. I wished to disappear.

"James? Casey?"

Cameras and mics were being shoved in my face.

"Get her out of here!" Cherry shrieked marching down an aisle lifting her satin train.

"It's Cherry's P.I. The detective to the stars!"

"Brittany, care to make a comment on the Donatus Sun case?"

"Brittany!" James and Casey finally reached me.

As we left the cameras continued to follow us out the door.

"Get me out of this!"

Casey and James blocked me as best they could all the way to the car. Standing at the passenger's side door I paused. Cameras flashed in all directions as I stood in front of my dad's black Impala flanked by the two tall men. I cleared my throat and the lot quieted down as if by magic.

"On Easter Sunday I was hired by Cherry Starlet to find her missing husband, Donatus Sun. We have reason to believe, hours and hours of tape recorded proof, that Donatus Sun was aided in his demise. We have proof that parts of Donatus Sun's suicide note were copied from letters he wrote to his record label, his promoter, and tour manager announcing his intentions to quit Bliss and leave Seattle, putting an end to a financial trajectory, resulting in the loss of millions. Kids are dying one copycat suicide at a time. We ask that Seattle PD re-open the case."

It took us forever to exit the crowded parking lot, cameras running alongside the Impala.

"Now if you get hit by a train, or get drunk and fall out a window people will blame Cherry's camp. Hopefully that buys some protection," Casey said.

"We're fired from the job for sure now." I'd done the right thing.

James was jazzed. The following week in the office we received phone calls from the poor to the rich to the celebrity class. It was a whirlwind of crazy. Insane, but a good insane. I'd gone to the press. The attention was off-putting, but being back in the office felt right. I felt grounded. The letter opener was a bit rusted. We should get a new. Hell, we should get a new everything. I carefully opened another letter.

"Hey, this one is from a thirty-two-year-old thanking us for helping him talk himself into getting help for his depression. That's early teens to people in their thirties who have written to thank us. It's hard to wrap my head around all these people considering suicide because of one man. One murdered man."

James nodded and took the letter I handed over.

"Do you think Casey would ever consider studying for the state licensing examination to become a P.I.?" I asked James.

I picked up the ringing phone. "Stacks Private Investigators, this is Brittany."

"Brittany, it's Cherry. I have another job for you."

211

ACKNOWLEDGMENTS

Thank you to my mentors, friends and family
for all their support.

Cover design by Cecilia Arthursson
Cover image used under license from Shutterstock.com
Secondary cover image: Sandsun/stock.adobe.com
Author photo © Kevin Francis Barrett

ABOUT THE AUTHOR

Adrienne Reiter writes books. Not on purpose. She holds an M.F.A. in Writing and Consciousness from the California Institute of Integral Studies and a philosophy degree from Mills College. "Ghouls Just Wanna Have Fun" is a paranormal podcast she co-hosts with Keri Schroeder of Coyote Bones Press. You can find them at ghoulsjustwannahavefun.com. A compulsive blogger, Adrienne contributes to Alex J. Cavanaugh's Insecure Writer's Support Group monthly. *Twist* and *Chosen* are the first in Adrienne's San Francisco-based Rebecca Ashley mystery novels series. She is known in the bay as a social media and communications specialist. Her articles have been featured in *Authors Publish* magazine and bayarea.com. A proud member of the Moscone dog walking group, Adrienne lives in San Francisco where her dog, Peaches, does bad things. Find out more and hit her up at adriennereiter.com and on Twitter and Instagram, @adriennereiter.